A MAGNOLIA HOMECOMING

THE RED STILETTO BOOK CLUB SERIES

ANNE-MARIE MEYER

For my friends

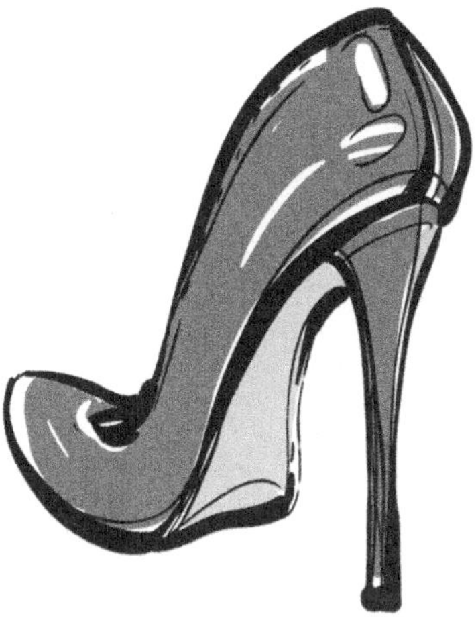

SHARI

"Bye, Mrs. Harper!" Hannah yelled as she hurried from her classroom and sprinted right past me. I raised my finger, getting ready to tell her to walk, but before the words left my lips, she'd rounded the corner and was out of sight.

I smiled as I shook my head. I didn't blame her. It was Friday. Everyone was desperate to get home. And the excited hum that sounded down the hallway told me there was no stopping the flow of students even if I wanted to.

So I leaned my back against the wall and nodded and waved as the kids passed by. Ten minutes later, the buses were gone, and the hallways that had thrummed with life were empty.

I sighed as I pushed off the wall and headed into the front office. Cassidy was sitting behind the front desk with her headset on, speaking loudly into the microphone that almost touched her lips.

"I know, Mrs. Trudue, but Lincoln is still here. He didn't get on the bus, and it has left."

I glanced over to see Lincoln Trudue sitting there with mussed blond hair and pink cheeks. I didn't have to ask to know what he had been doing instead of getting on the bus. "Playing on the playground?" I asked him as I rounded Cassidy's desk and pulled out the papers that were tucked in my mail cubby.

"No, I can't turn the buses back to come and get him, that's not how this works," Cassidy continued. I could hear the frustration in her voice.

I offered her a sympathetic smile, and she just widened her eyes. I chuckled. I knew the pain of dealing with parents who thought we had more control than we actually did.

Just as I opened my office door, Tag and Bella squealed. Bella was sitting on my desk chair, and Tag was spinning her around. I shut my door and walked over to set my mail in the basket on the corner of my desk.

"How was school?" I asked as I stopped the chair. Tag let out a growl of complaint. Bella looked green as she stumbled off the chair and staggered over to one of my armchairs opposite my desk.

"Mom, stop," Tag said with his newly adopted hint of annoyance as he pushed past me and back over to the chair I'd moved away from him. I swallowed the anger that rose inside of me. That tone was new, and I wasn't quite sure how to eradicate it. I knew it had something to do with the fact that Craig wasn't around much anymore.

Tag was not shy in informing me that I was not his father, and I wasn't sure how to handle his disrespect. As an educator, I'd attempted all of the responses I'd been taught in my training, but nothing seemed to work.

Apparently mother was different than teacher.

"I don't want you to spin in my chair. I have a few things to finish up before we can leave," I said as I kept my hand firmly placed on the chair. Tag stared up at me and then narrowed his eyes.

"Fine," he said as he grabbed his backpack and pulled open my door. He was gone before I could stop him. I sighed as I watched the office door close. Thankfully, the entire school knew who he was, and I trusted the other teachers to help keep him in line, even though it was completely embarrassing that I needed their help to do so.

I was his mother. I should know what he needed from me.

Feeling utterly exhausted, I collapsed into my now empty chair and tipped my head back and closed my eyes. I took in a few deep breaths as I allowed my mind to still. When it came to work, my life made sense. But once I stepped out of these four walls, everything fell apart.

And I was at a loss on how to pick the pieces up in any meaningful way.

"Tag's mad, Mommy," Bella said. I glanced over to see that she had her lunchbox open and was munching on some leftover animal crackers that I'd packed for her this morning. Her motion sickness must have worn off, and she was back to her happy, carefree personality.

"Yeah," I said as I straightened and moved to finish the emails I needed to send out and a few budgetary items I needed to record. Once I checked them off my to-do list, I packed a few projects into my bag and slung my purse over my shoulder.

Bella had finished her crackers and was now busy watching a show on my phone. Tag had yet to resurface.

"Come on," I said as I grabbed my empty water bottle and half-eaten lunch from my mini fridge. I'd been too stressed and busy to finish the leftover spaghetti I'd packed. In fact, my appetite had been pretty non-existent lately. Finding the lipstick stain on Craig's uniform three days ago hadn't helped.

I knew that things were bad between us, I just didn't know that they'd gotten that bad. When I confronted Craig about it, he claimed he had arrested a woman the night before. And I wanted to believe him, I did. But the pit that formed in my stomach told me otherwise.

I wasn't stupid, and it angered me that Craig thought I was.

I pushed thoughts of my husband from my mind as I grasped Bella's hand and walked through the office. I called a quick goodnight to Cassidy and pushed through to the hallway.

Thankfully, it didn't take me long to find Tag. He was holed up in the library with his nose tucked in a comic. He was predictable, that child of mine.

He sighed his annoyed sigh when I told him it was time to go. But I was grateful that he didn't push me too much. We piled into the car, and I drove through town to our home.

Mine and Craig's house. The one we'd bought when we were newly married ten years ago. The one we brought both Tag and Bella home to. The one that I couldn't help but feel was changing, and there was nothing I could do to stop it.

I pulled into the driveway, and Tag and Bella pulled open the doors and jumped out as soon as the car stopped. I allowed the engine to idle, cool air bursting from the vents and covering my skin. Goosebumps rose up in response, but I barely noticed.

Instead, I just sat there, staring at the closed garage in front of me. Our driveway was empty, which meant Craig wasn't here. Since it was his day off, I was expecting to find his car parked and him inside. But that wasn't the case.

"Where did he go?" I whispered to myself as I pulled out my phone and stared at the black screen. I had a sinking suspicion as to where he'd gone. Any woman knew when her relationship was slipping. But I didn't *know*, know. All my evidence was anecdotal, and I feared the backlash Craig would give me if I asked him.

So I drew in a deep breath and pushed out all the anxiety that had risen up inside of me. If I allowed my questions to eat me alive, I wasn't going to be the patient mother that my children needed me to be. Instead, I would be snapping at them for every little incident, and I couldn't do that to them. Not with Tag already sensing something was wrong.

Determination rose up inside of me as I turned off the engine and gathered my things. I slammed the car door and hurried inside. After dumping my purse on the table, I turned toward the kitchen only to silently curse.

Craig had promised to take care of the dishes today. But just like everything else lately, he'd failed to follow through. The dishes were stacked precariously in the sink, and I winced as I thought of all the dried food that was stuck to them.

My cheeks flushed as I fought the tears that clung to my lashes. I felt ridiculous, reacting this way. They were dishes. It wasn't like it was the end of the world. So why did it feel that way?

"Mommy, can I watch a show?" Bella asked, snapping me from my thoughts.

I startled and glanced down to see her holding up the family iPad. I nodded—even though I felt guilty—and turned it on. I needed all the help I could get. If I was going to get dinner cooked and the kitchen cleaned, I couldn't deal with the fights between Tag and Bella that were sure to come if I left those two to their own devices.

Tag was already in his room, and I could hear the sounds of his video games coming from under the door. I sighed, not liking what he was doing but feeling powerless to stop him. Craig had bought the gaming system despite my protests, and now if I took it away, I knew Tag would only resent me more. So I let him do it. I'd stop him eventually, but right now wasn't the time.

With both kids preoccupied, I turned my attention to the dishes. I grabbed my earbuds and slipped them in. I turned on our book club read and lost myself in the story as I unloaded the dishwasher. I was halfway through rinsing the dirty dishes and finding places for them when two arms wrapped around me, and suddenly I was airborne.

I screamed as I hurried to pull the buds from my ears. My first thought was for my children. But when I turned to see the big smile and floppy hair of Jake, my ridiculously childish brother, my reaction was stifled in my throat.

Jake chuckled as he set me down. I almost fell over but managed to catch myself before I did. Going from adrenaline pumping through my veins to relief left me shaky and unstable.

"What the crap, Jake?" I breathed out as I reached forward to whack his arm. He'd been planning to return to Magnolia earlier, but then a few of his traveling arrangements had fallen through. I'd been waiting to hear what had happened, but he hadn't sent me so much as a text. So I'd figured his plans of returning home were over.

He just stood there, smiling at me as he leaned against the countertop. He was wearing his signature t-shirt and jeans. There was a faint fish smell to him—one that I'd gotten used to over the years. And I would be lying if I said I didn't appreciate the familiarity.

It reminded me of home. It reminded me of our dad. It reminded me of a time when my life was a lot less complicated.

"I wanted to surprise you," he said as he reached out and grabbed a handful of grapes from the bowl on the counter. He popped one in his mouth and chewed for a moment before he grinned at me. "Were you surprised?"

I patted my heart for a moment, as if that was all it took to calm it down, and then returned to the sink where I grabbed the dish I had been rinsing. "What do you think?"

He nodded as he leaned into me. "I think you were terrified." He raised his hands. "*Ahh.*" His scream was much quieter and more mocking than mine.

I shouldered him but kept my hands on the dish that I then loaded into the dishwasher. Now that the machine was full, I added the dish detergent and pressed start. It hummed to life. With a now clean kitchen, I turned to face my brother who was busy finishing the grapes in his hand.

"How long are you here for?" I folded my arms and gave him an appraising look.

He chewed and swallowed before he spoke. "Until you get annoyed of me."

I sighed, needing his answer to be different. I needed him to be serious. I missed my brother, and right now, I could really use his support. "Seriously."

Jake held his smile for a minute before it fell. "Everything okay?"

I cleared my throat, frustrated that I'd let my guard

slip. I didn't want to burden him with my issues—especially when I didn't know if my assumptions were facts yet. So I smiled and nodded. "Of course. Your ancient sister just doesn't like surprises. I need to know what to expect. So I can *plan*."

Jake studied me for a moment before he chuckled. "Plan? What is that?"

I grabbed a dishtowel and swatted him with it. "It's what mature *mothers* do."

"Mother," he said quietly. Then he glanced around. "Speaking of that, where are my niece and nephew?" His gaze fell on me. "And Craig."

My cheeks flushed at the mention of my husband's name. And I knew that was ridiculous. I shouldn't react that way. But I had, so I turned to face the cabinet and busied myself with pulling down a glass as I gathered my emotions.

"Um, the off spring are getting screen time, and Craig had some things to take care of." I pinched my lips together as I waited for Jake to ask more. I knew my brother. He wasn't going to be satisfied with *I don't know*.

"Oh."

When he didn't say more, I turned to look at him. Needing to get my brother out of my house before he realized how crappy my life had become, I clapped my hands together. "I don't want to cook."

Jake raised his eyebrows as if I were asking him to do it instead.

I waved my hand in his direction. "That's not what I

meant. How about Shakes to celebrate you coming home?"

Jake's smile widened as he nodded and shot a finger pistol in my direction. "Genius. I'll grab my bag and stick it into the guest room."

My heart dropped. "The what? Why?"

He paused in the doorway. "Because I'm staying here until I find a place."

Before I could say anything, he was outside with the storm door slamming behind him. I stood there, gaping at the glass as our conversation played in my head like a toy monkey playing the cymbals.

Jake was staying here. In the house that was very quickly falling down around me. As much as I loved my brother, this was a part of my life that I didn't want him to see—that I didn't want anyone to see.

I felt like I was going to be sick.

This was not good. Not good at all.

2

CLEMENTINE

I sighed as I set down the book I'd been reading and arched my back. I'd spent the better portion of the last two hours trying to finish our book club read. The next meeting of The Red Stiletto Book Club was taking place tomorrow, and Maggie had made it clear that if I didn't finish, she was going to give me the stink eye— in the most loving way possible.

There was no way I wanted to be the only person in the group with nothing intellectual to add to the conversation. And since the formation of the book club had been my idea, it wouldn't look too good if I hadn't finished the required reading.

The bell on the door chimed, and I slipped off the stool and yawned as I slipped my book under the register. Two men that I didn't recognize walked into the store. I waved at them, and they acknowledged me and then headed down the screw and nail aisle.

Realizing that they probably didn't need my help, I focused my attention on cleaning up the random pieces of paper that cluttered the counter. Just as I dumped the scraps into the garbage, my phone rang.

I smiled when I saw that it was Maggie calling me.

Ever since she'd moved here two months ago, we'd become best friends. I guess it also helped that my brother, Archer, was her handyman and boyfriend. He lived in the small one-bedroom shack on the inn's property, leaving me to live in the apartment above the hardware store alone.

I swallowed as my emotions rooted themselves in my throat. I hadn't been this alone in a long time. Ever since admitting Dad into the memory care facility last month, I'd been attempting to get used to the silence that surrounded me every time I walked into the home I'd grown up in.

Once, it had been filled with laughter and love, and now, it was filled with only memories. That was probably why I spent most of my time over at Magnolia Inn, hanging with Maggie and Archer.

After all, there was no one missing me at home.

"Hey," I said into the phone as I stepped away from the register and over to the nearby aisle to organize the screwdrivers.

"Hey, Clem. Archer wanted me to see if you are coming tonight for dinner. He's going to put in an order at Shakes, and if you are coming, we were wondering if you could pick it up."

I nodded as I ran my finger over the newly straightened items in front of me. "Yeah, sure. I can do that." I clicked my tongue. "No luck in finding a chef yet?"

Maggie groaned. "Don't remind me. We're opening next week, and I have no idea what I am going to do if we don't have someone to cook. Heaven knows *I* can't."

"She can't." Archer's voice sounded muffled.

I laughed. "He's so mean," I said.

"He really is," Maggie said, but I could hear the admiration in her voice.

My heart squeezed. I was happy for my brother, I was, but I was jealous of the happiness he found. Everyone in my life seemed determined to leave me. Dad. Mom. Archer. *Jake.*

Jake Palmer. The only boy who'd been able to make me feel such happiness and, at the same time, such pain. He was the one that I'd been convinced I would spend the rest of my life with. I'd loved him and I thought he'd loved me.

But when the call to be a fisherman in Alaska came, our love wasn't strong enough. He wanted me to go with him and I wanted to stay here. So we said our goodbyes.

"Alright, well I'll let Brenda know you'll be picking up. See you at eight?"

"Yep," I said as I pulled my phone from my cheek and hit the end call button. Then I slipped my phone into my back pocket just as the two mystery men came walking up to the register.

After they paid, I said goodbye and they left. The shop

feel quiet once more, and just as I settled down to bury myself in my book once more, the shop door opened.

Max from next door came wandering in. He'd owned the hobby store for the last thirty years and had been one of my father's best friends. When Dad started to deteriorate, he'd helped us keep an eye on Dad.

"Hey," I said as I straightened and rested my elbows on the countertop. Max approached, tipping the brim of his hat up as he winked at me.

"Good afternoon, Clem," he said in his familiar booming voice.

I chuckled as the familiarity of his tone washed over me. He reminded me so much of Dad, and I couldn't help but feel nostalgic when he was around.

"What can I do for you? Your bathroom sink acting up again?" I asked as I moved to round the counter and head down the plumbing aisle.

When Max didn't move to follow, I turned to study him. His hand was up and he was shaking his head.

"I'm actually not here about that, surprise surprise." His eyes crinkled as he smiled at me. "I wanted to let you know that I'm selling."

I raised my eyebrows. "Selling?"

He nodded. "I finally bought that boat I've been talking about for the last ten years, and I'm going to retire on the ocean."

I chuckled and nodded. "Sounds about right." I was happy for him, I was, but I couldn't help but feel like everyone in Magnolia was moving on while I was still stuck here, in the hardware store, living everyone else's life but my own. "Well, I'm happy for you."

He grinned from ear to ear. "Me too. So if you hear of anyone who wants to buy the shop, send them my way. I'll give them a killer deal."

"Sure. Will do."

He patted my shoulder before he hurried from the shop. I watched him as he made his way past the front window and disappeared into his store.

Sighing, I headed back over to the counter and settled back down onto my stool. I stared out the window for a moment before I turned my attention back to the book I'd tucked away earlier.

I was happy for Max. Just like I was happy for Maggie and Archer. Here were three people who really did deserve true happiness. But I couldn't help but feel left out once more. Here was one more person who was living the life they wanted to live instead of the one that they were stuck with.

Tired of feeling pity for myself, I settled back and opened my book. I needed to stop focusing on my future or the lack thereof. There was no way I was going to be able to solve my situation by sitting around and stewing over it.

I needed to take care of my present. And right now, my present consisted of reading this book before tomorrow afternoon.

Once that was over, I would focus on the next task. And then the next. And I prayed that, eventually, all of these tasks would lead up to something that I actually wanted.

Because with the way my life was going right now, I wasn't happy. I wasn't satisfied. And I was beginning to fear that I never would be.

———

Time seemed to tick by slowly, and I was dragging when the clock struck seven thirty and I was able to close the store. I waved at Spencer as he stalked out of the back door. Now alone, I locked up and climbed into my car.

The drive to Shakes was uneventful. Finding a parking spot on a Friday night was less relaxing. When I finally found a small space that I could park my Corolla in, I sighed in relief. I pulled my keys from the ignition and shouldered my purse as I walked into the restaurant.

The smell of cheeseburgers and malt powder assaulted my senses. I closed my eyes for a moment as I breathed it in. There was nothing more relaxing in Magnolia than Shakes. It reminded me of my parents. It reminded me of home.

"Good evening, sweetheart," Brenda said, snapping me out of my reverie.

I turned to see her stick a pencil behind her ear as she walked up. She had a pad of paper in her hand and began punching the keys on the register. "Maggie's order will be ready in a few," she called over her shoulder.

I nodded and moved to the far corner so that I wasn't

in the way of the people coming and going. Once one of the chairs in the waiting area had been vacated, I slipped onto it before it could be taken away from me.

"Auntie Clem!"

I peeked around a few legs to see Bella run up to me. I smiled as I held out my arms and she jumped onto my lap. After a tight hug and a kiss on the cheek, she pulled back.

"Where's your mom?" I asked as I scanned the people that were milling around us.

Bella pressed on my cheeks, causing my lips to stick out like a fish. "She's waiting for Tag and Uncle Jake to get out of the bathroom."

The world around me faded away. All I could do was stare at Bella's lips as I tried to sort through everything I'd just heard.

Did she say *Jake*?

Bella didn't seem to notice my distress. Instead she continued to pat my cheeks and babble about school. I needed her to focus, so I pulled her hands way from my face and dipped down to meet her gaze.

"Who is your mom waiting for?" I asked.

Bella stopped talking and studied me. "Tag and Uncle Jake."

My stomach dropped. "Uncle Jake?"

I knew that he was supposed to come, but that was weeks ago. I figured that he'd changed his mind since I didn't hear anything else about it from Shari.

Apparently not.

"There you are," Shari said as she pushed through the crowd and stood over us.

"Hey," I said as Bella slipped from my lap and raced over to the gumball machine that stood by the register. I turned my attention to Shari, who looked exhausted. "Long day?"

Shari nodded and sunk down onto the chair next to me. "That would be an understatement." She closed her eyes and tipped her head back. "Thanks for keeping ahold of Bella. She slipped out of the bathroom before I could stop her."

Not sure how to approach what Bella had said with Shari, I cleared my throat and figured that treading lightly was the best move. "Did you guys come here for dinner?"

"Mm-hmm," Shari said with her eyes still closed.

Hmm, I was going to need to prod more. "Is Tag with Craig?"

Shari stayed quiet for what felt like an eternity before she cracked an eye and studied me. "No," she said slowly.

My entire body went numb as I waited for her to speak. But, before she did, the crowd parted and two very familiar blue eyes on a very familiar face came into view.

Annoyingly, my breath caught in my throat as I studied Jake. He looked older and, of course, dangerously gorgeous. Fate had quite a sense of humor, allowing him to show up in my life looking the way he did.

It wasn't fair that the man who broke my heart didn't have warts and a hunched back by now. Why did he have to be tall and slender and drop-dead ridiculous?

"Oh, Jake's back," Shari whispered.

I glared at her, and from the corner of my eye I saw Jake approach. He had his hand on Tag's shoulder and a very unreadable look in his eye.

I swallowed, forcing my nerves down as I turned to smile at him. It felt fake and forced and way too big for the occasion, but right now, I had no control over my body. My brain was firing randomly and nothing I was doing made sense.

"Hey," I said a bit too loud and a tad too shrill.

Jake's eyebrows went up, and my brain thought it would be a good idea to leap up from my chair and hug him.

Humiliation coursed through me as I stood there with my arms around his shoulders. Jake seemed as confused as I felt by my reaction, and I winced as he awkwardly patted my back.

"Hey, Clem," he said. His voice was deeper now and made my entire body long for the past. Long for the feeling of his arms around me for real. The feeling of him holding me like he never wanted to let go.

I missed that. And I hated that I missed that.

Not wanting to break down in front of everyone at Shakes *and* Jake, I pulled away and adjusted my purse, praying that Brenda would hurry up with our order.

"It's good to see you," I said, avoiding his gaze.

I saw him push his hand through his hair and nod. "You too." The silence that fell around us felt deafening even though the normal sounds of the restaurant filled the air. It was like my ears were trained to hear his voice, and the fact that he wasn't speaking killed me.

"You look good," he finally said, and those three words sent my heart off to the races.

Blast.

Luckily, like an angel in diner heaven, Brenda appeared, and I shot my hand up to get her attention. "Is my order ready?" I asked.

Brenda's eyes widened as she took in my desperate expression. "Let me go check, honey." I watched in horror as she slipped into the kitchen. I wanted to pull her back. I wanted to will our food into existence, but unfortunately, I didn't possess such powers.

Instead I was stuck standing right next to Jake, feeling completely unsettled. And I was frustrated because I knew exactly what that feeling meant.

"Bella," Shari called as she excused herself to run after her daughter, who had sprinted to the back of the restaurant.

Tag was hiding with a phone in his hand behind the Murray family, who were waiting for a table.

Even though we were surrounded, I couldn't help but feel as if Jake and I were very much alone. All of my senses were heightened, and I couldn't seem to ignore the fact that Jake Palmer was standing next to me with his blue eyes trained on me. Why did he have to be better looking with age? It wasn't fair.

"How're your dad and Archer?" he asked at the same time I asked, "How long are you here for?"

I pinched my lips together, and Jake studied me before extending his hand. "You first," he said.

I studied him before I offered him a small smile. "Archer's good. He found a job at the inn. And Dad…" My voice trailed off as a new kind of pain settled in my chest. "Dad went to a memory care home last month."

Jake's expression fell as my words settled in the air. "I'm so sorry," he said softly.

Not wanting his pity, or for him to learn just how warranted it was, I shrugged. "It's fine."

"Here you go, sweetie. Say hi to Archer and Maggie for me. I've got some family coming into town next week, and they are excited to stay at the inn," Brenda said as she approached me from behind with a paper bag in hand.

I took it from her and nodded. "Will do." I turned, and just as I did, I saw Jake reach out and grab my arm. Zaps of electricity shot across my skin from his touch. My breath caught in my throat and my entire body stopped as I stared up at him.

"It was good to see you, Clem," he said as he offered me a soft smile.

Not wanting to speak and have my voice give away how I was feeling, I just pinched my lips together, nodded, and hurried from the restaurant.

It wasn't until I was in my car with the door safely shut that I tipped my head back against the seat and let out the breath I'd been holding. Tears brimmed my lids as the memory of Jake and what we'd once had flowed through my mind.

I was angry that he left. I was angry that he stayed away. I was angry that he came back.

But most of all, I was angry that, despite all he did to me, I didn't want to be angry with him.

At all.

3

SHARI

Saturday mornings were supposed to be exciting. Or, at least, they had once been exciting. It was the day I had off of work, and, as he climbed the ladder at the department, Craig had off as well. We would spend the morning cleaning with the kids and then spend the afternoon hiking or going to the beach. The evenings would be filled with sipping wine on the porch and making love once the kids fell asleep.

But that wasn't the case anymore. Now, I found myself waking up alone once again. Craig was gone. He'd whispered to me that he'd taken an overtime shift in the wee hours of the morning, and I'd been too groggy to respond.

Now, with the sun seeping through the curtains into my room, I stretched out on the bed. My hand rested on Craig's pillow. I closed my eyes as happy memories assaulted my pain. I had been content once. There was a time when Craig and I had been in love.

But it didn't feel like that was the case anymore.

I was constantly finding myself alone, with Craig gone. And the fear of my marriage falling apart broke me more than I wanted to admit.

"You up?" Jake's booming voice followed three solid knocks on my door.

I sighed as I nodded and then pushed myself up. "Yeah, come on in."

The door opened and Jake was standing in the hallway with a bag of pancake mix in his hand. "I was thinking character pancakes for breakfast. What do you think?"

I chuckled. It was a Saturday ritual we would do as kids. We would wake up and have competitions to see who could make the best character out of the mix. We eventually got good enough that we entered our masterpieces into the Magnolia fair and won first place three summers in a row.

I quirked an eyebrow. "Think you still got it?" I asked as I pulled off the covers and planted my feet onto the ground.

Jake scoffed. "Are you serious? The guys on the boat were shocked that they had such a talented artist working among them."

I slipped a robe on over my nightgown and tied it as I followed Jake down the hallway. "Well I've been practicing when I can, behind closed doors, for this very moment," I said as we walked into the kitchen.

"Mommy!" Bella exclaimed. She was sitting at the bar, with her hair ratted on one side from where she'd slept on it. Her eyes were bright, and she hopped down from her seat and wrapped her arms around me. I gave her a kiss on the head before I started trying to comb my fingers through her hair.

"Owie," she said when my finger caught a snarl. She pushed my hand away, and before I could pull her back, she hurried back over to the stool she was sitting on.

I glanced around the room. "Where's the bear?" I asked.

Jake furrowed his brow. "Craig or Tag?"

I snorted. Lately that was an accurate description of the men in my life. "Tag."

Jake chuckled as he grabbed a bowl from the cupboard. "I checked on him, and he's still sleeping." He paused and I felt his gaze on me. "I found the TV on." His words drifted off, and I knew what he wanted to say.

I sighed, not wanting to have this conversation right now. We'd grown up in an anti-tech house. Our parents had forced us to live outside. So my son having a TV in his room was not what I wanted. But Craig had given it to him, and I couldn't take it away. I was tired of fighting when I had no one backing me up.

"Yeah," I said as I busied myself with getting out the griddle and helping guide Jake to everything he needed. I hoped if I kept our attention on breakfast, Jake would forget what he so obviously wanted to say.

Soon the batter was mixed, and we poured in into squeeze bottles. I flicked water onto the griddle, and it popped in response.

"It's ready," I sang out as I wiggled my eyebrows in Bella's direction. She giggled and nodded. "I'm thinking...Elsa?"

Bella cheered, pumping her fists in the air. I smiled as I started drawing the outline of Elsa. Was it weird that I could picture her face in my mind as I drew?

Probably.

Once she was drawn, I waited a few seconds before flipping her over. Bella oohed and aahed over the pancake while Jake wiggled his way passed me so he could have full control of the griddle and started drawing Olaf.

We laughed as we made up a few more pancakes that included a Star Wars themed one for Tag whenever he rolled out of bed. Then we drizzled some syrup all over them and headed to the table to eat.

Jake told us fishing stories, and Bella and I stared at him as he acted out the time he caught a great white shark. Bella's eyes were wide, and syrup was dripping from her dropped jaw. I sipped on my coffee as I chuckled at her reaction.

Sure, Jake was flighty. He ran, full speed, away from Clementine when things got serious. He'd been young and stupid, and because of our parents' divorce when he was in high school, he feared commitment.

"I don't want to hurt her," he told me as he shoved his clothes in Dad's military-issued duffel bag the night he left Magnolia for good. I tried to stop him, I did, but he wouldn't listen.

Fear does that to a person. Blinds them to what is good

for them and convinces them they want something different. I tried to stop him, but he was determined. And my brother is an unstoppable force when his mind is made up.

The laughter died down, and soon, the only sound was the clinking of our forks on our plates. I dragged the last bit of Yoda's face though a pile of syrup and slipped it into my mouth. Then I grabbed the handle of my mug and leaned back.

After a few sips, I glanced over at Jake, who had grabbed another pancake and was slathering it in butter.

"So, what's your plan for Magnolia?" I asked, giving my brother my best big-sister stare.

He paused his chewing to meet my gaze but then picked up again. I could see the muscles of his jaw working. I wondered if the exaggerated movement was how he ate now, or if he was just prolonging our conversation.

I steepled my fingers, resting my elbows on the table to signify I wasn't going anywhere. He was going to answer my questions. Partly because I cared about him. And partly because I couldn't have him living in my house forever. Life with Craig was unstable, and the more Jake hung around, the more he would discover.

And right now, there was no way I could handle his questions or sympathetic stares.

After he swallowed, Jake took a long drink of his milk and then set his glass down. After a quick swipe at his upper lip, he glanced over at me. "I've got plans. I have some money saved up to help me for the next few months if that's what you are worried about."

This was positive. I liked seeing my brother be responsible. I furrowed my brow. "Who are you and what did you do with my kid brother?"

Jake let out a burp and I wrinkled my nose in disgust. Bella just giggled, bouncing up and down on her knees as she knelt on her chair.

"Oh, never mind, there he is," I said as I picked up my napkin and threw it his direction. He laughed as he caught it and then crumpled it into a ball.

I grabbed my plate and utensils and balanced them on my arm as I picked up my mug and finished the last sip of my coffee. Then I brought the dishes over to the sink and set them inside. After rinsing them, I loaded them into dishwasher and then filled up my mug for one more sip of coffee.

I was probably going to be jittery all day, but my to-do list was as long as my arm, and with the book club meeting tonight, I was going to need all the energy I could get.

Tag came walking into the room, dragging his feet and rubbing his eyes. I sighed as I bit back the urge to lecture him. We were drifting apart, and me constantly being on his case wasn't helping matters.

"Morning," I said as I began to load up a plate for him.

Tag didn't respond as he walked right past me and over to the table, where he pulled out a chair and sunk down onto it. I swallowed, hating that my son didn't respect me and that I felt helpless to change it.

"Your mom said something to you," Jake said. My gaze snapped over to him, and I watched as my brother poked my son's shoulder.

Tag glowered at Jake as his lips tightened. I knew that stance. I'd been on the receiving end of it one too many times. The excitement of having his uncle home must have worn off, and in a way, I felt kind of glad that Tag was treating Jake like this. It told me I wasn't the only one.

I hurried to pour syrup on the pancakes and drop Tag's plate in front of him. With the stare-down that was happening between the two of them, I feared one of them wouldn't come out alive.

"Say thank you to your mother," Jake said in a tone of voice I didn't recognize.

It caused a shiver to rush up my spine. I didn't like it. It made me feel helpless and protective at the same time. I shouldn't need someone else to parent my child. I should be able to do it myself, and my husband should be here, helping me. None of this was Tag's fault. It was mine—I was the one unable to keep control of my child.

"It's fine," I hissed as I passed by Jake.

He grabbed my arm, halting me in my steps. I glanced down at him with pleading in my gaze. This wasn't the time to have this argument. I wanted to have a semi-decent day. If it started with an outburst from Tag, then my errands and chores wouldn't get done because I would be so focused on defusing the bomb that was my child.

If Jake cared about me and the situation I was in, he would drop the conversation like I so desperately wanted him to do. Jake's eyebrow went up as he studied me, and then he sighed, nodded, and dropped his hand.

Relief flooded my body, and even though I could tell that he wanted to talk about this more—this was not the last time I was going to hear from him—I was glad that, for now, we'd tabled this discussion.

Jake focused his attention on Bella, and soon they were laughing and rinsing the dishes. Jake even poured some soap into the mixing bowl, and they were having fun trying to create the biggest bubble. Tag had eaten and left the table in favor of his room. I watched as he walked away, wanting to call out to him to have him stay and hating how helpless I felt.

"Why don't you go shower? Take some time for yourself."

I glanced up to see Jake offer me a sympathetic smile.

My entire body instantly felt heavy from his reaction. Apparently my ability to hold up the curtain over my disaster of a life was slipping. If Jake saw my inadequacies, did everyone else? Not being able to handle the disappointment I felt in myself, I nodded and wrapped my arms around my chest in an effort to protect my heart as I headed up to my room.

Once I got inside and shut the door, I slumped against the wall and let out my breath. I closed my eyes and stilled my emotions as they began to suffocate me. How had things gotten to this point? How had things gotten this bad?

A few years ago, I would have never imagined my life getting to this point. I always thought things were going to be happy forever. I found Craig. We had Tag and Bella. There was nothing more that I could ask for…until now. Now it felt like my life was slipping away, and there was nothing I could do about it.

Pushing off the wall, I headed into the bathroom and turned on the shower. As steam filled the room, I slipped out of my pajamas and into the hot water. My skin turned pink from the heat, but I reveled in the relaxation as my muscles were massaged by the pressure of the water.

I allowed my tears to mix with the water. The shower was the only place I allowed myself to cry. After all, no one would hear me. And if they saw me after, they would only assume my red eyes were from the shower. It was my place of solitude where I let out all my stress and worry. Carrying it all day, every day, was too much.

I cried for five minutes before I angrily wiped away the tears and got started on cleaning my hair and body. After the last of the suds were rinsed down the drain, I turned off the water and stepped out of the shower. I wrapped a fluffy towel around my body and busied myself with getting dressed and doing my hair and makeup.

Once I was somewhat presentable, I opened my bedroom door only to find Jake in the hallway, with one shoulder resting on the wall and his arms folded across his chest.

I yelped and gripped my heart as I hurried to shut my door behind me. For some reason, I knew that if my brother saw my bedroom and the lack of Craig's presence, it was only going to be further proof to him that something was indeed wrong.

"You scared me," I said as I reached out and shoved his shoulder.

Jake chuckled as he pushed off the wall, his six-foot-three frame towering over me. It had been a strange day when Jake grew taller than me. For so long he'd been my little brother, and even though that was the still the case in age, it was no longer the case in stature.

He met my gaze, and I could see the questions floating around in his mind. He studied me in a way that made me feel raw and exposed. And I didn't like the feeling.

At all.

How dare he force me to confront the things that I had been living with every day since the moment I smelled someone else's perfume on Craig's shirt. Or saw the lipstick stains on his collar. *I* was living this life and trying to make it good. How dare he want to discuss anything with me.

I wasn't going to have it.

"I have things to do," I said, my tone sharp and to the point. He needed to understand that I knew my life sucked. I didn't need his judgement on my handling of the situation.

"Shar—" He grabbed my elbow, but I snapped it away as fast as I could.

"I have things to do, Jake. I don't have time to stand around and talk." Those blasted tears clung to my lashes, and I would be damned if I allowed my brother to see them. I didn't need his pity, just like I didn't need his solutions.

I needed to get out of here and to the grocery store, where I could find some normalcy in my day. Once I got there, I would feel better. I would feel safe.

Because right now, I felt anything but safe. My home was no longer my haven.

My home was my prison.

4

CLEMENTINE

I flipped to my side and pinched my eyes closed. I counted down from ten and slowly let out my breath. I relaxed my muscles as I attempted to force sleep to come. But as I lay there on my bed, trying to force sleep, nothing happened.

I was still very much aware of the sun streaming into my room, the clicking of the clock on the wall, and the fact that Jake Palmer was back in Magnolia.

Groaning, I pulled my covers over my head. I lifted my hands and feet up to tent my blankets.

"Why?" I asked to the daisy flower print on my bedsheet. Mom bought these sheets for me a year before she passed away, and even though they were old and worn, I couldn't bring myself to throw them away.

I reached out a finger and traced the edges of one of the flowers. Then I sighed and pulled the covers off my head and stared up at the ceiling. The white paint that I'd used a few years ago when I'd scraped the texture off the ceiling was yellowing. It definitely needed a fresh coat.

Like my life. My entire life needed a fresh coat of paint.

I stumbled into the bathroom and spent entirely too long under the hot water. So much so that when an icy cold blast of water hit my damp hair, I yelped and flailed, knocking over my shampoo in an effort to turn the water off. I cursed as I grabbed towels to wrap around my hair and my body. I ignored the mirror as I padded out to the kitchen to start the coffee machine.

I glanced at the clock, and my heart picked up speed. It was 10:05 which meant Spencer was already here and most likely annoyed that I was making him wait. Not wanting to face the wrath of Spencer, I grabbed my keys and hurried down the back stairs and into the store. I made my way across the floor and over to the front door.

Spencer was standing there next to the glass door with his typical annoyed expression on his face. I unlocked the door and gave him a sheepish look.

"I'm so sorry," I said as I stepped out of the way so that he could come inside.

He grunted a response and headed straight back to his shop.

I sighed as I stood in the open door, staring out at the street. This was my life. My giant, crappy life. Standing in a towel, staring at the world as it moved around me. It felt unfair but accurate. Why did I expect anything else would happen?

My gaze drifted to the street, and I noticed few empty bottles of beer. Not wanting something like that to deface the storefront that my father had worked so hard to build, I walked the few feet out onto the sidewalk and picked them up. Just as I did, someone cleared his throat.

My entire body froze as that sound washed over me. I straightened, gripping my towel closer around my body. All feeling. All thought. All ability to form any type of sentence flew from my mind when I was met with the half smile and laughing eyes of Jake Palmer.

"Hey, Clem," he said in a way that sounded as if he were asking a question.

My eyes widened as I parted my lips. I needed words to come out of my mouth, but not even a hint of sound squeaked out. That only caused Jake's eyebrows to rise higher on his forehead.

"Everything okay?" he asked.

When his gaze traveled over me and then settled back on my eyes, my entire body flushed with heat. I tightened my grip on my towel as I took in a deep breath.

"I had to unlock the door for Spencer," I said. When my wheezy and shaky voice hit my ears, I pinched my lips together.

What was wrong with me?

Jake bobbed his head up and down slightly. "Ah. Makes...sense." He then cleared his throat as he glanced around and pushed his hands through his hair, causing it to stick up.

I couldn't help but stare at it as the desire to reach out

and smooth it overwhelmed me. I shook my head slightly in an effort to free those thoughts from my mind. There was no reason for me to even think like that anymore. Jake wasn't mine, and from the words he'd said to me the night he left, he never would be.

A car drove by, snapping me out of my reverie. I cleared my throat and straightened as I eyed Jake. This street was my street. Why was he even here?

"Did you come to see me?" I asked, hoping that he would buy the lie of confidence that I was trying to peddle.

He chuckled and shook his head. "Um, no. I'm here to talk to Max." He waved toward Max's hobby store.

I furrowed my brow. "Why?"

Jake shoved his hands into his front pockets and shrugged. "He's renting out his apartment above the store, and I'm in the market."

I stared at him, my lips parted. I was trying to form a sentence in my mind to express how I felt about this situation, but nothing came out, and I feared that I looked like a fish out of water with the way my lips were moving.

Embarrassment coursed through me as I clamped my lips shut and regained my bearings. "He said that? I thought he was selling the store."

Jake nodded. "He's selling both but looking for a renter until he finds the buyer." Then he clapped his hands together before he jutted a thumb in the direction of the store. "Well, I should get going, and I'm guessing this isn't the new uniform for the store," he said as he waved toward my towel.

I glowered at him as I tightened the towel around my body. I didn't appreciate his teasing, no matter how adorable it made him seem. I wasn't going to forgive him. I couldn't. Not if I wanted to survive. Not if I wanted to make sure I didn't fall for him like I knew I was in danger of doing.

No longer wanting to stand on the sidewalk, showing my unshaven legs to all of Magnolia, I hurried back into the store. I passed by Spencer's counter to see him setting things up for the day.

"I'll be right back. Hold down the fort for me," I sang over my shoulder. I didn't wait for his response as I sprinted up the back stairs and into my apartment.

I pulled on a yellow spring dress, ran my fingers through my damp hair, and put on a touch of mascara and lip gloss. Once I looked *and you gave this up* good, I slipped on my strappy sandals and headed downstairs.

Spencer didn't look happy when I joined him behind the register, but I didn't let that sway me from the wide smile and kiss on the cheek that I gave him. He harrumphed and headed to the solitude of his corner.

There were a few people picking up items, so I hung around the register to answer any questions. Time ticked by, and I didn't notice that it was noon until my stomach rumbled. I pressed my hand to my waist and realized that I never ate breakfast or drank my coffee.

Thankfully, most of Magnolia seemed to have food on

the brain, and the store stilled. I rustled around in the drawers behind the counter until I found a granola bar. I didn't bother to check the expiration date because there was no way I wasn't going to eat it—ignorance seemed best in this situation.

Just as I pulled the wrapper halfway down the bar, the bell on the door jingled, snapping me to attention. I sighed when I saw Shari walk in. This was why I hated that Jake was back. He infiltrated my brain when he shouldn't be there.

Like now, for instance. Every time I saw Shari, I knew I was going to panic that Jake was right behind her. I was going to prep myself to see him even if he never showed. My simple life was going to become drastically more exhausting.

"Hey," I said as I rounded the counter to get a better look at who would be coming in behind her. Tag and Bella? Jake? If he was coming into my store, I needed to be prepared.

"You look nice," Shari said as she lifted up a plastic bag with the Shakes logo printed across it. My mouth instantly watered at the thought of a juicy hamburger and greasy fries.

"Number seven?" I asked as I moved back behind the counter. If Shari was coming with sustenance, I didn't care who else she showed up with. All I needed was the artery-clogging meat to satisfy my hunger. She could bring the devil with her and I wouldn't care.

And right now, Jake was pretty close to being my personal devil.

Shari laughed as she nodded and set the bag on the counter. We tore into the food, and it wasn't until my stomach felt as if it were going to burst, that I finally came up for air. I licked my lips and then took a long sip of my strawberry shake.

"You are amazing," I said as I gave her a wide grin.

Shari chuckled. It wasn't until I was no longer stuffing my face that I realized she'd barely touched her roast beef on rye. Instead, she was just picking pieces off her fries and slipping them into her mouth.

I set my shake down and turned my focus to her. I was a terrible friend to not notice that she was struggling with something. I'd been too focused on Jake's return and my need for food.

"What's up?" I asked as I leaned forward and caught her gaze with my own.

Shari glanced at me, and I could see from her far-off look that something was bothering her. "Hmm?" she asked, raising her eyebrows.

I held my gaze. "You haven't touched your sandwich. I don't think there has ever been a time when you *haven't* devoured your roast beef on rye." I tapped my forefinger on the counter. "Out with it. You can tell me."

Shari shifted as she let out a nervous chuckle. "It's nothing. I'm fine," she said in a way that made me realize she was most certainly not *fine*.

I studied her before I straightened and took another sip of my shake. There were two things I knew about Shari. One, she was a terrible liar. And two, she was a people pleaser. If something was bothering her, the last thing she wanted to do was weigh down the listener with her issues.

If I was going to wiggle it out of her, I needed to be strategic in my efforts. So, for now, I was going to drop the direct approach. "Okay," I said softly, hoping she would realize that I'd heard her and was going to respect it. "Ready for tonight?" I asked as I dunked a fry into my shake and then shoved the whole thing into my mouth. The taste of sweet mixed with salt hit my taste buds, and I couldn't help but close my eyes in happiness.

Shari sighed, and when I opened my eyes, I saw her shrug. "I'm almost done with the book. I probably won't finish, but at least I can add something to the conversation." She winced. "Hopefully Maggie won't hate me."

I laughed and shook my head. "Maggie won't hate you."

Shari nodded as she slipped a fry into her mouth. "Good to know."

I crumpled up my napkin and set it in the Styrofoam container. Then I closed the lid and shoved it back into the bag that Shari brought the food in. "Where are Tag and Bella, and how did you know that I needed this?" I asked as I held up the bag.

Shari chuckled. "Well, I know how busy you get on the weekends, and I was at Shakes." She stretched her arms out in front of her. "And Tag and Bella are with Jake. He was apartment hunting earlier, but now he's taking them to the arcade for some uncle bonding time."

I swallowed. All of the greasy, sugary food I'd just consumed sat like a rock in my stomach. I cleared my throat and pushed my straw around in the melted remains of my shake. "Jake's back," I said. The words came out a whisper, and I wasn't really sure if I'd uttered them or just thought them or if they were really true.

"Yeah. It surprised me too. I would have given you more of a heads-up if I'd known. But you know my brother, that kid does love making an entrance." Shari set her sandwich down in its container and closed the lid. She wiped her fingers on a nearby napkin and smiled over at me. "But it's okay. It's not like you're still hung up on him or anything," she said with laughter in her voice.

I cringed. She knew so little about my heart, and really, that wasn't her fault. I wasn't big on sharing my lingering feelings for Jake with her. After all, she was his sister and my best friend. There are some lines that you don't ask your friends to cross. And picking sides between me and her family felt like one of those lines.

"Yeah. It was just a shock," I said as I slurped the last of my shake and then tossed the cup into the garbage behind the counter. "A heads-up would have been nice, but it wasn't like I had no clue that he was thinking about coming back. You did warn me there."

Shari nodded. "True. And maybe it's for the better. It's time you move past him and start dating." She wiggled her eyebrows like that was the solution to all of my problems.

I groaned as I picked up all the stray napkins and chucked them into the garbage on top of my empty shake cup. "Dating and me. Bleh," I said, shaking my head.

Shari chuckled. "Yeah, dating…" I waited for her to add more, but nothing else came. Her face had fallen, and she was staring a bit too hard at the countertop in front of her.

An awkward silence fell around us, and I studied her for a moment before I glanced around. The secrets that Shari was holding were becoming more and more evident every time I spoke to her. Something was going on. Craig was doing something—or not doing something—and it was bothering her.

I just wished she'd open up to me about it. Then I could help her. If not, I was at a loss, floundering, as I watched my best friend struggle. It was an awful place to be.

"Hey, things will be okay," I said as I reached across the counter and patted her arm.

She twitched as if she wanted to pull away, but she didn't. Instead, she sighed and nodded as she gathered the food bag into her hand. She shouldered her purse strap and glanced up at me with a tight smile. "I'll throw this in the dumpster on my way out," she said as she held up the bag.

I nodded and offered her a sympathetic smile, deciding not to hide the concern I had for her. I wanted her to know that I saw her hesitation and that I was here to help if she needed. "Awesome. I've got some lightbulbs to organize," I lied as I walked toward the aisle.

"See you tonight?"

"Yep," I called over my shoulder. "I'll see you tonight."

I paused in the middle of the lightbulb aisle, waiting to hear the sound of the front door opening and closing. Once silence engulfed the store, I sighed and fiddled with the filament bulbs that were hanging next to me.

Not only did I have Jake's sudden appearance to contend with, I also had the withdrawal of my best friend. And I couldn't help but feel helpless in both situations.

I swallowed and rubbed my temples as I pushed out my deflated feelings. Right now, I needed to finish up here and then head on over to Maggie's. Maybe by the time I saw Shari next, I would know what to say.

Maybe then, I would have a solution to our problems.

5

SHARI

"A book club?" Craig wrinkled his nose as he sat down on the chair in our master bedroom. He rested his ankle on his knee as he began to untie his shoe. He looked more awake and refreshed than I'd expected him to.

Well, I wasn't sure what I expected anymore. I was so surprised when he came walking through the door right after I got home with Jake and the kids that I almost spilled the chocolate milk I was pouring for Bella.

Thankfully, I caught myself before the kitchen became a milk lake and hurried to twist on the lid for her water bottle—that girl is all thumbs and no fingers—before handing it over to Bella.

Jake gave me a few moments to compose myself by stepping up to Craig and shaking hands. Craig kept his distance—he'd never really liked anyone from my side of the family—by standing a few feet off and keeping his responses to Jake's questions short and to the point.

It made me angry when I saw Craig walk away from Jake when Jake was mid-sentence, but what could I do? The last thing Craig would approve of is me pointing out his rude behavior. So I threw an apologetic smile in Jake's direction and hurried off after my husband.

Now, he was sitting in our room, pulling his shoes off and looking at me like I was a crazy person for wanting to go to a book club.

"I told you about this on Monday, Wednesday, and last night." I managed to keep my voice even. It was taking all of my strength not to snap at him. I knew we had our issues, but they would only be exasperated by me losing my cool.

Craig sighed as he put his now shoeless feet on the ground and leaned back against his chair, steepling his fingers. His eyebrow was quirked as he stared at me. "Since when do you read books?"

I was leaning against the wall on the other side of the room, and without its support, I would have fallen over from his response. *Since when did I read?* What kind of question was that?

"Well, if you were home more often, you might see what I do," I spat out before I could stop myself. For a moment, I allowed my true feelings for Craig and his *job* to rear their ugly head.

From his widened eyes and stoney expression, my intention had not been lost on him. He knew exactly what

I'd said and why I'd said it. He cleared his throat and shifted in his seat so that his elbows were now resting on his knees. He tipped his head forward, and I could see his breathing deepen by the way his shoulders rose and fell.

"Everything I do, I do for you and the kids," he said slowly.

The cadence of his voice and his tone sounded like molasses in my ears. My skin crawled from the sensation of it. I never really knew how to take him when he was like this. It was like he was manipulating me, but I was never really sure.

When he spoke, it left me feeling raw and exposed. But was that from me being too sensitive or was there something deeper happening here?

"I know, I'm sorry," I said like a reflex. I'd gotten used to apologizing. I was doing it a lot lately.

He didn't answer right away, and all I could do was stare at him, waiting for his response. All of my senses were on high alert. My muscles were poised to pounce or withdraw. I was truly in fight or flight mode.

What was he thinking? Was he angry?

"I'm going to shower and then go out with the guys," he said as he stood and walked past me without stopping.

I watched with my lips parted as he slipped into the bathroom and shut the door. It wasn't until the pipes squealed on that I let out the breath I'd been holding. I blew it out, allowing my lips to vibrate from the force. I closed my eyes and leaned my head against the wall.

Of course he was going to go out. His life was always

more important than my own. How could I possibly have a book club when he needed to head to Anchor Point Pub for some time with *the guys*?

My stomach felt hollow, and it ached inside of me. I wrapped my arm around my waist as if that was the only way to hold my life together. Physically stopping the mess I felt inside gave me a sense of control when everything else felt far from my grasp.

Realizing that Craig wasn't going to be interested in discussing this further when he got out, I glanced at myself quickly in the mirror and headed out to the kitchen. Jake and Bella were sitting at the table, playing some game on his phone. Tag was nowhere to be seen, but his door was shut, so I figured he was in there.

Jake must have heard me coming because as soon as I stepped into the room, his gaze was on me.

"Everything okay?" he asked as he handed his phone over to Bella, who happily took it.

I forced a smile and shrugged. "Yeah, why?"

Jake's eyebrows rose as he swept his gaze over me. Then the sides of his lips turned down as he shook his head. "No reason. Just…" His voice trailed off, and it caused the heat to rise on my neck.

I swallowed as hot tears pricked my eyes. I was desperate to keep my emotions in check, but that ability seemed to be a distant memory right now. All I could think of was the fact that Craig was here and, in a few minutes, would be leaving again. My marriage was probably on its way out, and I was going to be left more alone and more downtrodden than I'd been in years.

Was I really that unlovable? How could a man go from promising to love me and create a world with me to not wanting any part of it? Our family was a burden for him now, and it left me wondering if it had been something I'd done.

A mistake *I* had made.

I gathered myself together enough to face Jake, who was still watching me like I was a ticking timebomb about to explode. "Hey, are you busy tonight? I've got a book club I have to go to, and Craig has a meeting with some guys at work." I offered him a smile, and I hoped he would take it as truth rather than the lie that it was.

Jake narrowed his eyes. "Meeting with the guys? Where? Anchor Point?"

I groaned as I made my way over to the fridge to grab out a water bottle. I cracked the lid and downed half of it before I screwed the lid back on and turned to face him. I thought washing down some ice-cold water would help relieve the frustration that I felt, but it did not.

My annoyance toward my brother was now at an all-time high. It was taking all of my strength not to snap at him. "Jake, I don't know. It's for work, so what can I do?" I gave him a pleading look. I needed him to stop poking around in my marriage. I was barely hanging onto the threads as it were. If he kept asking, I was sure the last few strands would snap, and I would fall, fast and hard, into the unknown.

He stepped back as if my words had slapped him. He stood there with his jaw clenched. I could see his muscles twitching as he studied me. He wanted to say something but was battling with himself.

Finally, he ran his hands through his hair and nodded. "Yeah, sure. Of course I can watch the kids. I'm thinking we do pizza and a movie tonight. Does that work?"

Relief flooded my body as I nodded. I loved my brother, and I hated the secrets that I had to keep from him, but I couldn't tell him. Not when I hadn't exhausted all avenues to help myself first. This was my marriage. It was my job to see it through to the end.

"Thanks," I said as I finished my water, crumpled the bottle, and tossed it into the recycling. "I'll be back around nine to take over."

Jake had moved back and was now leaning against the table with his legs extended and his arms folded across his chest. "Yep," he said with emphasis on the *p*.

I shouldered my purse, kissed Bella on the top of her head, and shouted a goodbye in the direction of Tag's room. Then I waved at Jake as I tucked my stilettos under one arm and dug my keys out of my purse with the other. I was in a hurry, not because I was late, but because I was worried that Jake would change his mind or that I would have to face Craig. And right now, I didn't want to see either of those men.

After stopping by Sand Dollar Bakery and picking up the dozen sugar cookies that I'd promised to bring, I headed over to the inn. As I turned off the engine, I glanced around the parking lot. It was sparse to say the least. I winced as I worried about Maggie. This weekend was her soft launch, and from the looks of the turn out, it probably wasn't going well.

With the cookies in hand, I slammed the driver's door and headed up the front steps. The warm ocean breeze washed over me, filling my senses with the smell of salt water and freedom. I took a second to pause and inhale.

There was something soothing about the beaches of Magnolia. Things were simpler by the ocean. It moved at a slower pace than anywhere else on the island. I envied Maggie and the fact that she now lived on the beach. This was her reality.

I smiled as I pulled open the front door, and the sound of laughter carried out from the living room on the left side of the house. I slipped my sandals off and my red stilettos on. Then I rounded the corner to find Maggie and Clementine standing by a small refreshment table, dipping carrots into some dip.

I nearly fell over as I walked up to them. I used to rock stilettos—really any shoe—but after Bella, my feet felt like boats that I was never able to get off the ground.

"Shari," Maggie exclaimed as she wiped her fingers on a napkin and reached out to take the cookies from me. "Let me take that."

I watched as she set them down next to Clementine's to-die-for brownies. "That's wholly unfair," I said as I grabbed a grape tomato and popped it into my mouth.

Clementine laughed as she licked some dip off her fingers. "What? My brownies?"

I gave her a playful glare. "No one can contend with your brownies. You should have told me that you were bringing them. I would have at least attempted to make my cookies look homemade." I jutted my finger at the white box that Maggie had just opened.

"These look amazing," Maggie said. I'd had Janae draw a red stiletto with icing on the cookies, and she'd done an amazing job.

"Janae is the queen of baking," I said as I munched on a carrot.

We all murmured in agreement.

"Well, don't you ladies look so fancy," Archer's voice boomed, and we all turned to see him saunter into the room. He wore a tool belt with a hammer and drill hanging from it. His shirt was damp—no doubt from working out in the sun all day. He laughed as he reached out and snapped up a brownie before Clementine could swat his hand away.

"This is for the ladies of the book club only," she said as she waggled her finger in Archer's direction.

"I'll join," Archer said after biting half of the brownie off into his mouth.

Maggie laughed. "Stilettos are a must," she said, waving toward her feet.

Archer chewed thoughtfully as he studied her feet for a moment. Then he swallowed and took Clementine's distracted moment to grab another brownie. "Never mind, I think I'm good." He dodged Clementine's fist, hunching over the brownie like it was a coveted football, and scurried from the room.

"Yeah, you better run," Clementine said. She started taking after him but then almost tripped on the rug, so she stayed rooted to the floor. Once she'd regained her balance, she glanced back at us sheepishly and then gingerly walked over to join us.

"It's good to see that you two have grown up," Maggie said. The affection for Archer in her voice made my heart ache.

I remember feeling like that once for Craig. The feeling of absolute joy. The thought that there would be no other person who could complete you like they did. There was this soul completing feeling that you couldn't get anywhere else.

When you found your soulmate, that was it. All the questions in life were answered. You were no longer alone but with someone who cared for you as much as you did them.

It was a feeling I'd had once, but now I was beginning to doubt I'd ever felt it. And the hope that I still had it was dwindling like a fire trying to outlive a rainstorm.

My efforts felt futile and heartbreaking.

Other members of the book club started to arrive, and I found myself bouncing from conversation to conversation, having surface talk, but not really diving into anything deep. Everyone seemed to be doing well, and I was beginning to wonder if I was the only one who felt as if their world was floundering.

I felt like I was desperately trying to walk up the wrong escalator. No matter how much I attempted to fight against the current, there was no winning. I was on a path that I no longer had any control over.

All of my smiles, all of my fake attempts at laughter, left a hollow feeling of emptiness in my chest and cast a lonely shadow over my soul. Was I the only one that was hurting? Was I the only one that doubted my own future?

That thought scared me more than anything had in a long time. The not knowing what was going to happen to me—to my family—crushed me.

Thankfully, Maggie was good at directing the conversation and I was allowed to linger in the back, just listening to the discussion between everyone else. Once in a while, I caught Clementine studying me as if she were trying to figure something out, but when I met her gaze, she startled and flashed a quick smile my direction before turning to respond to Maggie.

I sighed as I pinched the bridge of my nose. Even though I wanted to believe that I was fooling the people around me, I knew that wasn't true. People were starting to suspect something, and if I didn't act fast, I would soon be bombarded with questions. I was going to have to face the reality that I was getting pretty dang good at ignoring.

And right now, I wasn't ready for that. I wasn't ready for everyone's advice about what I should do. As much as I hated what Craig was doing to me, I had Bella and Tag to think about. It was no longer what was best for me, it was now what was best for my family. I couldn't behave rashly.

For all I knew, Craig really was spending all of his free time at work. I could very well be jumping to conclusions.

Even though the pit of my stomach told me otherwise, I needed to cling to the thought that my marriage—my family—may be salvageable.

At least, for now, I needed that hope.

Hope was what could save my family, and that was all I cared about.

My family.

6

CLEMENTINE

I wanted Shari to stick around after the book club meeting, but she was gone before I was able to catch up with her. Victoria said that Shari got a call and excused herself. I had half a mind to ignore what Victoria said, but when I texted Shari and she responded with the same evasive explanation, I had no other choice but to let it go.

Well, let it go as much as I could. I had questions for Shari, and they were burning inside of my gut. When I sighed and set down my glass of wine on the small side table, Maggie chuckled and pulled the blanket she'd wrapped around her shoulders tighter.

"Feeling okay?" she asked as she tipped her head back and closed her eyes.

We were sitting on two of the five wooden rocking chairs that Maggie had specially made in Newport. They rocked so smoothly and effortlessly that they made you feel as if you were on the ocean instead of dry land.

I groaned as I brought my feet up to rest on my seat and propped my chin up on my knees. I stared out at the moon as its light danced across the ocean. The sound of the waves lapping at the shore was like a mesmerizing song that my heart sang along with.

Magnolia was so engrained in my life that every aspect of this island felt like a part of me. All I had to do was move farther down the road and a familiar sound or smell would come over me and I would be transported back to a memory that I associated with that sensation.

It helped me feel grounded and in control—which were a few things I was sorely lacking nowadays. Without Archer and Dad, I was incredibly alone. And it was getting harder and harder each day. The fact that I was losing Shari as well was killing me. I needed her to open up to me.

I needed her to trust me.

"I'm worried about Shari," I said softly as I drew circles on the wood beneath me.

From the corner of my eye, I saw Maggie lean in. "You're worried about who?" she asked.

I sighed as I straightened and turned to face her. Maggie seemed startled that I moved as quickly as I did, and she pulled back, her eyes wide.

"I'm worried about Shari."

Maggie settled back into her chair, pulling her blanket up to her chin. Even though it was the beginning of May, the breeze off the water and the lack of sun had a way of chilling a person.

"Why are you worried about Shari?" Maggie asked.

I chewed my lip as I stared out at the water. I wasn't sure how much Shari wanted others to know—and if I were being honest with myself, I didn't know very much—so I wasn't sure what I could say. I contemplated that for a few seconds before I pushed those thoughts from my mind and decided it was best to just be honest. After all, Maggie had gone through a divorce. She could give me some good advice on how to handle this situation.

I turned to face her with a serious expression. Maggie must have picked up on it because, a moment later, her smile fell and she furrowed her brow. "Everything okay?"

Realizing that I might be giving the wrong impression, I smoothed out my expression and nodded. "Yeah, sorry. That might have been a little more intense than I wanted." I laughed.

Maggie chuckled nervously as she nodded. "Good, cause you were freaking me out a bit." She relaxed into her chair and reached out to run her fingers across the weave of the blanket. "So, what's up?"

I grabbed my wine glass and rested the stem on my leg. I pushed off against the deck, allowing the chair to rock a bit before I straightened and turned to face her. "I'm worried about Shari and Craig."

Maggie's eyebrows went up. "What's wrong with Shari and Craig?"

I sipped my wine for a moment before I set it back

down and turned to face Maggie. "I think something is going on between her and Craig...that's bad," I spoke last few words like they were a secret. I cringed at the idea that I might be gossiping about my friend, but I was truly at a loss as to what to do with her. It wasn't like she was freely offering me information.

Every time I even attempted to bring it up, she shut me down. I wasn't gossiping, I was discussing for her benefit. How could I help her if she wasn't going to talk to me?

"Like, divorce-type somethings?" Maggie was slowly rocking back and forth on her chair as she stared out toward the ocean.

I sighed. The cloud that had settled in my heart only confirmed what she was saying. "Yes," I said quietly.

Maggie tsked as she took a sip of her wine. "Poor Shari," she whispered.

I nodded. I felt the same. "What can I do?"

Maggie tipped her head and met my gaze. "Has she talked to you about it?"

I shook my head. That was a question that hurt me to my core. My best friend couldn't talk to me about something as big as this. "No. If I even attempt to ask, she shuts down."

Maggie's gaze softened as she got a far-off look in her eyes. As if she were reliving something through my words. "I can relate. It took me a while to admit what Sean was doing." She straightened her head so that she was staring out at the ocean once more. "Sadly, there's not a lot you can do if they aren't willing to acknowledge it."

She ran her finger rhythmically around the rim of her glass.

I hugged my chest as I contemplated her words. I knew that what she said was true, it was just not something I wanted to acknowledge at this moment. I wanted to think that I could help Shari. I'd already lost too many people in such a short amount of time, I couldn't bear the thought of losing another one.

"I'm sorry," Maggie said.

I nodded and downed the rest of my wine as I leaned back in my chair. I closed my eyes for a moment before I turned to face her. "It's okay. I get it. I'll wait until Shari's ready." I gave her a soft smile.

"Shari's lucky to have such a great friend looking out for her. When Sean left me, I relied on Brielle to keep me sane. Right now, all Shari needs are friends."

And that was what I could be. I just wished there was something more. Something I could do to help lessen the load she carried.

Needing to change the subject, I glanced over my shoulder at the inn. "How's the soft launch going?"

Maggie groaned. "Don't remind me. I'm grateful we did the book club because it let me take my mind off the complete failure I fear next week will be."

I reached out and patted her hand while giving her my best sympathetic smile. "It'll go great, I'm sure of it. Plus, Archer'll help, right? He won't let you fail."

Maggie pinched her lips together and nodded. "Archer is a godsend. If it weren't for him, I'm pretty sure I'd lose my mind." She sighed, and I could see the love she had for my brother wash over her expression. It made me happy for her. They both deserved happiness.

"I'm glad to hear that he is being helpful and not a hinderance."

Maggie chuckled and then glanced over at me. "What about Jake? You were all up in arms when you saw him yesterday. What's the story there?"

At the mention of Jake's name, my stomach sank. I forced a smile and a shrug, but from the crease that appeared between Maggie's eyebrows, she didn't believe my response. So I sighed and shook my head.

"We have a history. I loved him. He left. End of story." I glared at my wine glass, angry that I'd wasted the wine by drinking it in one gulp. If we were going to have the Jake conversation, I needed some liquid courage to ward off the pain that I knew was going to strike me down.

When Maggie didn't respond, I peeked over at her to see that she was studying me. Her eyes were wide and her lips parted into an *o*. I winced when I realized how she must have taken my response. She was just trying to be nice, and I had to go and jump down her throat.

"I'm sorry, Mags," I said, offering her an apologetic smile.

Maggie laughed and shrugged as she tipped the final sip of her wine into her mouth. "You're preaching to the choir. I'm sure I responded to many people the same way when they asked me about Sean." She rested her glass on her leg. "It just means you loved someone deeply and were hurt deeply. Nothing wrong with that." She glanced over at me and met my gaze. "Just don't let it ruin you. At some point, you either need to face it or let it go. Holding onto anger does nothing for your soul."

I swallowed, knowing that what she said was true, but I couldn't believe that I could experience it for myself. How does one get over a broken heart like that? Especially when the one who broke it is living and breathing in your space? It was easier to forget Jake when he wasn't around. But now that there was a chance that I could run into him, all of the old feelings were rising to the surface and turning my once calm life into a boiling mess.

"I understand," I said, suddenly feeling drained. It had been an emotional day, starting with Jake seeing me in my towel, moving to Shari and whatever she was keeping from me, and now this conversation with Maggie. My nerves were not ready to be exposed and repeatedly rubbed against like this.

I need a bed to crash on and soon.

Maggie must have sensed my exhaustion because she stood and took my glass from me. "Come on. You're staying the night."

I parted my lips to complain but stopped when she narrowed her eyes and gave me a *you're gonna* look. When I realized that I didn't have a choice, I just stood and shuffled after her.

The room she set me up in faced the ocean. The walls were a pastel blue with sand-colored sheets. There were pictures of sand reeds that she'd purchased from a local artist. It was simple but beautiful. I loved the detail that Maggie put into the light fixtures on the side tables—a dark brushed gold—and the leaf ceiling fan above me.

Everything spoke to a getaway, and instantly, my nerves seemed to settle.

After a hot bath with some of the complimentary bath salts, I slipped into a pair of pajamas that Maggie brought me and crawled into bed. As soon as my head hit the pillow, I was out. My entire body relaxed and darkness took over.

I startled awake the next morning, rubbing sleep from my eyes and glancing around. Thankfully, I'd had enough sense to shut the drapes last night, and from the darkness of the room, they were effective—or I'd just woken up in the middle of the night.

Glancing over at the time, I groaned. I hoped it was still night because if it was ten in the morning, I was late opening the hardware store, and Spencer was going to have a field day with me when I finally got there.

I'd offered to make him a key, but he said he didn't feel comfortable. I had a sinking suspicion that it had to do with his past, but if I tried to ask, I knew he'd just shut me down. So I bit back my questions and made sure I arrived on time every day to open the door.

I flung my covers from my body, padded over to the

drapes, and yanked them open. Sun streamed into the room, causing me to shield my eyes until they adjusted.

Crap.

It was morning, and I was late.

I grabbed my clothes from yesterday and shoved them into my purse as I located my shoes that were strewn across the room and headed to the door. Just as I pulled it open, Maggie appeared in front of me with a breakfast tray clutched in her hands. She startled as she took me in.

"Where are you going looking like that?" she asked, nodding toward my hair, which I was sure was a matted mess right now.

I closed my lips, which were hanging open, and finished pushing my purse strap up onto my shoulder. "I gotta go open the store," I said as I tried to sprint past her.

Instead of letting me go, she moved to stand in front of me, blocking me with her body. I stared at her, wondering what she was doing and trying to figure out why her smile was so big.

"Archer went to take care of things," she said as she moved toward me, effectively pushing me back into the room.

It took a second for her words to register, and when they did, all the adrenaline that had been coursing through me settled, leaving me feeling shaky and disoriented. I moved to the bed and collapsed on the edge.

Maggie followed me in, setting the tray down next to me. She chuckled as she uncovered the plate. The smell of eggs and toast wafted up. "Archer wanted to give you a break. Eat breakfast, get ready, and then come downstairs."

I nodded, still staring at the food and feeling incredibly thankful to Maggie and Archer. I'd felt so alone these last few weeks, and with one sweet gesture from my new friend and my brother, suddenly I didn't feel so alone anymore.

Maggie patted my shoulder as she left the room, shutting the door behind her. I sat for a few seconds longer before I turned, settled onto the pillows, and pulled the tray over my lap.

The eggs were delicious. I wasn't sure if I was just extremely hungry or if Maggie was secretly a Michelin star chef, but the food tasted amazing and I was a tad disappointed when I glanced down to find that the plate was empty.

Feeling much better now that I'd eaten something, I climbed out of bed and decided to take a quick shower to help tame my out-of-control mane. By the time I got out, Maggie had left me a soft summer dress to wear. I pulled it on, along with my sandals and purse, and headed out of the room.

The inn was quiet as I headed down the stairs and into the kitchen, where I found Maggie sitting on a barstool at the island, sipping on a cup of coffee. She had her phone out and was laughing at something.

I grabbed a mug and poured a cup for myself and then settled down next to her. She straightened and glanced over at me. Her eyebrows went up. "Feel better?"

I nodded as I sipped the steaming liquid. "Yep, thanks to you."

Maggie reached out and gave me a one-armed hug. "I'm happy to hear that. I feel like it's sort of my job to help the people that come to Magnolia feel content and satisfied."

I chuckled. "Well you definitely did that." I held my mug between both of my hands, feeling the heat emanating from it.

Maggie's smile spread across her lips as she got a very contented look on her face. I could tell that this was where she was supposed to be. Compared to the woman who first came here, she was more confident and more satisfied. And I was so happy that she'd found her place in the world.

If only I could find mine.

"Wanna go to Newport and do some shopping?" Maggie asked as she turned off her phone and laid it flat on the counter.

I gave her a smile and nodded. "Let me call Michelle in to relieve Archer, and then we can go when he gets back."

Maggie clapped her hands and cheered. The oven rang, and Maggie slipped off her stool and padded over to open the door and pull out a tray of cookies. I sat there, sipping on my coffee and allowing my mind to wander.

I was incredibly happy for my friend because she had found what she wanted to do with the rest of her life. She'd found the man she wanted to spend her time with and the field she wanted to work in.

But I couldn't help but feel helpless about my situation.

As much as I wanted to hope, I was beginning to doubt my happily ever after existed. It was a possibility for others but not for me.

I was destined to be alone in that hardware store—forever.

7

SHARI

My nerves were even more rattled when I woke up this morning than they had been last night when I got home from the book club.

Spending a few hours staring at perfectly happy women laughing and chatting while I sat off to the side had made me feel completely hopeless about my life. About my ability to be happy again. And then Craig came home, smelling of alcohol and perfume. He tried to climb on top of me, and I had to wrestle him off. Sex had been taken off the table back when I found lipstick on the collar of his shirt. Which he seemed to be okay with—until he was drunk. Then he didn't care.

Thankfully, it only took one shove for him to roll over and pass out on his side of the bed. I lay there, staring up at the ceiling, listening to him snore and hating him for it. I just wished he would be honest with me for the first time in his life. I felt like he was still hanging onto me while living a separate life.

It was confusing and hurtful, and it only angered me more.

2 a.m. rolled around, and I finally got up and joined Bella in her bed. I felt safer there than in the same bed with Craig. Bella was small and warm and snuggled up to me like she did when she was an infant.

With my arms wrapped around her, I drifted off to sleep only to be awoken by her bonking my head with her own. I winced as my eyes flew open to see Bella's wide eyes.

"I'm sorry, Mommy," she said softly as she reached out and gingerly touched the spot on my head that she'd hit.

I gave her a soft smile. "It's okay, sweetie."

Bella moved to sit and stared down at me. "Why are you in my bed?"

I pushed up to sitting and turned to study her. "I had a nightmare."

Bella's eyes widened. "Was it scary?" she asked, her voice low with concern.

I reached out and pulled her onto my lap, where I began to run my fingers through her long hair. "Very scary. But being next to you helped me feel better." I worked out the snarls in her hair while she swept her hand over her comforter and hummed.

My heart ached for my daughter. I wanted a good life for her, and I couldn't help but feel like I was failing on all fronts.

My kids meant the most to me, and I wanted to give them all the happiness they deserved. I had a sinking suspicion that leaving their father was counterproductive to that desire.

I tied Bella's hair up into pigtail buns, and as soon as I finished, Bella sprinted off my lap and changed into a Frozen dress. She then proceeded to spin and twirl in front of her mirror.

I laughed and shook my head as I climbed off her bed and straightened. All the joints in my body whined, and I stretched in response. Never had I felt so old and disconnected with my body than I did right now. It felt like everything was out of my control. I was getting older. My marriage was falling apart. My relationship with my son was struggling. The life I once had was no longer a reality for me.

And every day that passed without me confronting Craig was a day that I wasn't truly living.

Bella's sudden kiss on my cheek pulled me from my thoughts. I startled and moved to see her grinning up at me. She patted me on my head while saying, "It's okay, Mommy. You don't need to be sad."

I paused for a moment when I realized that, to my daughter, I looked sad. I forced a smile and pulled her in for a hug. I tickled her sides and caused her to squirm. She squealed with laughter and finally wiggled off my lap and away from my reach.

I climbed off her bed, and we went out into the hall to find Tag emerging from his room. I met his gaze and offered him a smile, but he just grunted and disappeared into the bathroom.

I sighed, trying to figure out when my nine-year-old had suddenly turned into a moody teenager. He was too young to be behaving this way.

Bella grabbed my hand and dragged me into the kitchen, where Jake and Craig were sitting on opposite sides of the table, not talking. The tension in the room was palpable, and I was desperate to defuse the situation before it exploded into something I couldn't control.

"Morning," Jake said as he reached his arms out for Bella to jump into them. She didn't miss a beat as she leapt onto his lap and proceeded to eat his cereal—despite his laughing protests.

I busied myself with making some oatmeal, all the while keeping my attention on Craig, whose expression was hardening as he kept a side-eye stare on Jake and Bella. I knew he didn't like my brother—or anyone in my family. And I knew that, later, I was going to hear him complain about Jake's presence.

"How long are you planning on staying here?" Craig finally asked. His jaw muscles were tight, and I could see them twitch. I could only imagine how hard he was biting down.

Jake paused and raised his gaze up to meet Craig's. He took a bite of his cereal before speaking. "Shar?" He turned to face me.

I was startled by him addressing me. I straightened and glanced over at him. "Yeah?"

"I got the place over Max's hobby shop. So I'll finally be out of your hair." He winked at me. "That'll make you happy."

I peeked over at Craig, who was back to scrolling on his phone while eating a doughnut. He didn't look as irritated as he'd been a few seconds ago, which was a relief. "That's awesome. When do you move in?" I asked.

Jake leaned back in his chair and bounced Bella a few times on his lap. "He said as early as this afternoon. He's still looking for a buyer for his shop, but until that happens, he's more than willing to live with his daughter off island." He met my gaze. "So whenever you want to get rid of me, I can leave." His eyes widened, and I could tell he was attempting to open up a dialogue that I wasn't really ready to have.

"This afternoon would work. The kids and I can help." I tried to ignore the hurt in Jake's gaze as he digested my words.

I could tell that he wanted me to open up. He knew something was going on that I wasn't talking to him about. But I couldn't talk about it. If I did, I feared that I would break more than I already had. Besides, I had every intention of fixing my marriage, I just needed some time. And having my kid brother hanging around, making my husband uncomfortable, was not going to help that situation.

Desperate to put a positive spin on Jake leaving, I clapped my hands. "Doesn't that sound fun, Bella? Helping Uncle Jake decorate his apartment?"

Bella cheered while Jake said, "Decorate? Who said anything about decorating?"

I laughed, but when the legs of Craig's chair scraped against the floor as he suddenly stood, I pinched my lips shut. He looked so frustrated, and if we hadn't been struggling like we were, I would have felt bad for him.

He looked lost, and that tugged at my heartstrings. I never wanted to displace anyone. Not like this.

"Craig," I said as I moved to follow him.

"I'm going to the range," he shot over his shoulder as he headed out the back door. The sound of his engine starting as he pulled out of the driveway filled the silent room. I stared after his car, wishing that I could somehow pull him back here.

Bella's wide eyes and her tiny quivering lip made me angry that her father acted this way. She deserved better than this. I hated how, whenever things got complicated, Craig just left.

"What color do you think I should paint my room?" Jake asked as he pulled Bella's attention over to him. "Green? Yellow? *Pink?*" With his final word, he pulled her toward him and wiggled his eyebrows.

That seemed to be all she needed to pull her back, and she giggled and told him that pink was for girls and he wasn't a girl. He thanked her for her help and told her he'd be lost without her here.

I distracted myself with eating my oatmeal even though my stomach felt like a rock. Exhaustion was taking over my body and mind, and I wasn't sure how long I was going to be able to last like this. Craig was a volcano that was about to erupt, and I was spending my life waiting for that to happen. The anticipation was nerve-wracking and left me feeling weak and deflated.

Tag finally joined us at the table, and even though he kept to himself, it was nice to have him next to us, not looking completely annoyed. Jake and Bella filled the silence with their plans for a tree house in his apartment, and this allowed me to relax as I listened. It gave me something to think about other than my marriage.

Once breakfast was cleaned up, I got into my van—the kids chose to ride with their uncle in his truck—and we headed across the bridge to get some sheets and household items that Jake didn't have.

When we left the store, my van and the bed of his truck were full of items. I rolled down my window as I drove back to Magnolia with my hand out the window and music blaring from my speakers.

I rested the other hand on the bottom of the steering wheel and leaned my head back to relax against the headrest. I focused on my breathing, taking deep breaths and then slowly releasing them. Just the sheer calm that filled my mind caused my entire body to relax. All of the stress that I'd felt earlier today was gone, and all that existed was me and the road.

This was what I'd needed.

We stopped by Shakes to pick up our order and then headed over to Max's hobby store and parked behind the building. The kids were out of Jake's truck before he'd turned off the engine. Bella was jumping up and down while Tag followed after Jake, who'd just got out of the truck and was making his way to the tailgate to lower it.

I watched as my son had a longer conversation with my brother than he'd had with me in the last six months combined. It had been a long time since I'd seen my son like this. Awake and full of life. It almost made me want to beg Jake to stay with us. I hated taking Jake away from my son when he has this effect on him.

I sighed as I shook my head and pulled my keys from the ignition. It wasn't fair to Jake to expect him to step in where Craig should be. Jake was back in Magnolia to establish his life, and I doubted that included taking care of his sister and niece and nephew. Jake was a single guy who wanted to live a single life.

But he was nice enough to allow his needs to come second. And I needed to keep that in mind. If I asked him for help, Jake wouldn't say no. Instead, he'd stick around, giving up on opportunities that came his way, just to protect me.

And that wasn't fair. Dumping the results of my poor decisions on my brother was the last thing I wanted to do. So I was going to pull up my big girl panties and face my problems head on.

I opened my trunk and pulled out the comforter set and the bags of towels. Bella came over and grabbed the lava lamp that she'd picked out for his room. Then we followed Jake as he unlocked the back door to the stairs that led to the apartment.

It wasn't anything special, but it was clean. The wallpaper and kitchen appliances definitely spoke to another time. Max had lived here for decades, and even though he'd taken good care of this place, it looked as if he'd never updated it.

"Wow," Jake said as he set down the lamp he was carrying and spread his arms out, twirling in the empty living room. "This is mine?" he asked. His grin was wider than I'd ever seen.

"Feel like you're getting your land legs?" I asked as I nodded to his shorts. Jake had always been a water child. He'd lived in the ocean more than on land as a kid, so it was strange to suddenly see him so content with staying on solid ground instead of in a home that rocked with the movement of the waves.

Jake pinched his lips together and gave me a mysterious smile. He chuckled as he picked the lamp back up and headed toward the back of the apartment, where I assumed the bedroom was. I followed after him with so many questions pelting my mind.

What was that look? What did it mean? Did he seriously want to settle here? What was his game plan?

It was strange to see my brother like this, and I needed to make sure that aliens hadn't abducted him and replaced him with a species that was determined to wipe out life as we knew it.

"Jake," I said as I cornered him in his room. His eyebrows went up as I stared into his eyes. I searched his gaze for a moment and then narrowed my eyes as I stepped back. "Who are you and what did you do with my brother?" I asked as I folded my arms.

Jake shoved his hands into his front pockets and scoffed—taking his time to look everywhere other than at me. "I don't know what you are talking about," he said when he finally returned his gaze to mine.

I jutted out my pointer finger and jabbed him in the shoulder. "You want to stay here and, dare I say, put down roots?" I narrowed my eyes. "Why?"

Jake rubbed his shoulder for a moment before he lowered his hand and leaned into me. "Who said I'm giving up on the ocean?"

I pointed to the ground. "You're getting an apartment on land, happily. This is very much not normal for you." I studied him. "If you're a hostage, blink three times, and I'll find a way to save you."

Jake lowered himself to my level and stared into my eyes. He remained very still and, a second later, he blinked once…twice…and then shoved my shoulder. "You're crazy. I thought you'd be happy to see that your kid brother was growing up."

I studied him, and then a smile, relaxed and natural, emerged. Without analyzing my actions, I reached out and pulled him into a hug. He held back for a moment, but then he wrapped his arms around me and hugged me back.

Tears picked my eyes as he held me for a moment. When we pulled back, he was studying me. I could tell that he wanted to ask me what that was about. He wanted to know what was wrong. I wasn't ready to have that discussion, but I wanted him to know that I would come to him when the time was right.

"I'm okay," I said before he got the words out.

He furrowed his brow, and my expression morphed to one of desperation. I didn't want to lie to him. I wanted to keep my feelings the way they were right now. I wasn't ready to speak ill of Craig, no matter what I thought he was doing to me.

I wasn't ready to walk away from my family, and if I started discussing my issues, that seemed like a snowball I wouldn't be able to stop once it got rolling. I could feel Jake's hesitation, but then he nodded and moved to stand next to me. He brought up one arm and wrapped it around my shoulders.

"Well, know that I'm here, sis. Anytime you need me, day or night, I'll be here. I'm not planning on going anywhere anymore. Magnolia is my home now."

I nodded and slipped my arm around his waist. We stood there, and I could feel his support for me. We were just two siblings with the other one as our only support.

A spark ignited in my chest when I realized, for the first time in a long time, I felt a little hopeful. I was beginning to feel as if happiness was within in my grasp.

And for the first time in a long time, I felt at peace.

CLEMENTINE

My alarm woke me up a little too early the next day. After Maggie and I spent the day shopping, we had dinner at the inn, courtesy of Archer, and then I drove home feeling tired but happy.

Maggie had been right—this was what I needed. A day when my troubles didn't exist. A day when I could let my hair down and just feel happy. It was beautiful, and if I were honest with myself, I didn't want it to end.

So waking up in my bed on a Monday morning, knowing that the only thing I had to look forward to was working at a hardware store alone, and then coming home to an empty apartment, caused the dark clouds of disappointment to roll in. The sunny feelings that came from yesterday were gone, and reality was big, fat raindrops falling on my emotions.

I pulled my pillow out from under my head and

pressed it into my face. I took in a few deep breaths and let out my scream. I closed my eyes and allowed my frustration to hover over me. After all, what else could I do? It wasn't like I could be happy. What was there to be happy about?

I was alone, and I was pretty sure I was destined to be alone forever.

I whimpered in an exaggerated manner as I pulled off my pillow and covers and stood. I shuffled over to the bathroom and flipped on the shower. Once the water was hot enough, I entered, allowing the pressure to beat on my muscles.

I tipped my head back, and the water washed over my face, helping me to relax. Just as I reached forward to grab my soap, icy cold water sprayed onto my face. My entire body reacted, causing me to suck in my breath and lean over to smack the water faucet to the off position.

Once the feeling of nails against my skin was gone and I'd successfully hawked up all the water that I'd taken in, I leaned against the shower wall and took in a few breaths as I tried to calm my adrenaline.

Well, that was *not* the way I wanted to spend my morning.

After testing the water a few times to see if the hot water had returned, I finally resigned myself to the fact that I wasn't going to shower today and got out. I wrapped a towel around my hair and body and headed into my room.

I dressed and braided my hair, all the while telling

myself that I couldn't get upset over this. I had such a good day yesterday, and I didn't want to ruin that with a crappy Monday morning.

10 a.m. rolled around faster than I'd anticipated, but I was okay with that. Work had a way of distracting me, and I was ready for that distraction. I opened the front door to the store and found Spencer waiting for me. He didn't say anything as he passed by me and headed into his little corner.

"Good morning," I sang out to him. Perhaps if I acted like a Disney princess, I would feel like one too.

If Spencer heard me, he didn't turn around to respond. I just smiled at his back and headed out to the front of the store to make sure that there wasn't garbage scattered around. As I did, I hummed to myself, allowing my frustrations to melt away as I danced down the sidewalk to pick up a Styrofoam cup.

Then I spun and danced down the other side to pick up a plastic bag. My soul felt free as I hummed and twirled around the sidewalk. I was pretty sure that I looked like a crazy person, but I didn't care. I needed to relieve my stress, and this was the best way to do that.

Dancing had a way of transporting me to a place where my struggles and worries didn't exist. For a moment, the only things that mattered were my feet, the music, and the movement of my body. I could be...free.

I'd finished picking up the garbage, but I didn't stop dancing. For a moment, during a spin, I caught sight of myself in the window of Max's store. I paused, staring at my reflection. I looked happy, and I hadn't looked that way in a long time.

Suddenly, an idea began to formulate in my mind as I stared at the empty store in front of me. It wasn't huge, but it just might be the right size for a dance studio. I cupped my hands and peered further inside.

I'd put mirrors along the farthest wall with a barre. There could be a small receptionist desk by the front door, and if I removed all of the shelves and storage places, it would make for an amazing dance studio.

My heart was pounding as I pulled away from the window. I was trying to calm my emotions, but they wouldn't slow down. Instead, my excitement coursed through me like an unstoppable train.

I wanted to open a studio. Even if I hadn't danced in years, it didn't mean that dancing no longer existed inside of my veins. It was a part of my soul, and I couldn't ignore it anymore.

I sprinted into the hardware store and over to the computer. After fishing out my phone from my back pocket, I located Max's number in the business registry that we'd put together a few years ago as a sort of neighborhood watch strategy. I punched his number into my phone.

I pressed it to my ear and attempted to still my pounding heart as I listened to it ring.

One. Two. Three—

"Hello? Max's deep voice boomed.

I smiled, my grin now taking over my entire face. "Hey, Max. It's Clementine."

"Hey, Clementine. How can I help you?"

I cleared my throat to attempt my most convincing voice. "I was wondering if you have been able to find someone to buy your store."

Max was silent for a moment, and I closed my eyes as I waited for him to dash my dream. Was I a fool to hope that I just might be able to finally do what I wanted?

"I have someone who's interested but hasn't pulled the lever yet to make it official. Why do you ask?"

I blew out my breath. That was good news. It meant I had a chance. "I'm interested in taking it off your hands."

"Really?"

I nodded as if the physical act of agreeing gave me more confidence. It did not. I still felt like the little kid that had grown up next to him. I wanted him to take me seriously, but I feared that he wouldn't. "Yes. I need to talk to the bank and figure out the logistics, but I first needed to know if it was still available."

Max laughed. It was deep and rich and reminded me of Dad. For a moment, I longed to hear Dad's laughter again. I made a mental note to stop by to see him when I got off of work.

"Well, Clem, I'm open to selling it to anyone who writes me a check. If you can get everything in order, let's talk."

I nodded as I reached out and fiddled with the stack of receipts next to me. "I will. I promise." I paused before speaking again. I wasn't sure if it was my place to ask, but I needed to know before I went through all the work of getting a loan. "Can you wait until I come with an offer?"

Max was quiet for a moment. "Sure. I can do that. I'll wait to make a decision until you put your offer in."

I pumped my fists in the air but managed to stifle the cheer that was building up inside of me. That would only confirm to him that I was still the child he knew.

"Thank you," I said.

"I'll give you until the end of the month."

"That's reasonable. I will get it to you as soon as I have the number in hand."

"Perfect. I'll look forward to it."

We said our goodbyes. After hanging up, I tossed my phone onto the counter and did a little dance around the store. For the first time in a long time, I was actually excited about something. It felt as if my life was changing—and changing for the better.

The front door opened, and the bells chimed. I didn't stop dancing as I moved toward the entrance to greet my first customer of the day. Just as I spun out of an aisle, two firm hands wrapped around my upper arms, and a deep, familiar voice whispered, "Whoa," in my ear.

My entire body froze when I realized that Jake was not only standing in the store, but holding onto me. Zaps of electricity rushed across my skin, making me feel shaky. For a moment, I remained there like a deer in headlights, but once my senses caught up with me, I pushed away from him.

"I'm sorry," I murmured as I brushed down my shirt and raised my gaze to his. His lips were tipped up into a smirk, and it was all I could do not to glare at him. I cleared my throat and glanced around the store. "Did you need something?"

Jake pushed his hands through his hair, and for a moment, he looked unsure. Which was strange. Jake had been a confident guy for as long as I knew him. For him to be rattled, rattled me.

The seconds he took to respond to me felt like the longest seconds of my life. I studied him, waiting for him to speak. He seemed just as discombobulated as I felt. And that did nothing for my nerves.

"I was just stopping by to say hi and grab some lightbulbs. There are a few that are out in my apartment."

I blinked a few times. I hadn't expected any of those words to come out of his lips. It took him dipping down to meet my gaze for me to snap out of my daze and focus on what he'd just said. Lightbulbs—I could handle that. Apartment? That made me confused.

"Lightbulbs are down here," I said as I waved for him to follow me. I tried not to notice how close he was as he walked behind me. Or the fact that he smelled and felt so familiar.

My body had done a horrible job at forgetting the guy I wanted it to forget, and that angered me. It was like I'd learned nothing from him leaving. I was a glutton for punishment apparently.

"Here you go," I said as I nodded toward the shelves of

lightbulbs that I'd organized the other day when it was incredibly slow. I stood off to the side, not wanting him to feel like I was staring over his shoulder but also not wanting to leave until he explained what he meant by *my apartment*.

I was just taking my time in figuring out the most tactful way of doing it.

"Do you have any recommendations?" Jake asked as he picked up a box and then set it down again.

"What do you mean by *my apartment?*" The words spilled from my lips before I could stop them.

Jake paused and glanced over at me. Then he slowly turned his attention back over to the lightbulbs. "I'm renting Max's apartment next door."

My eyes widened as I took a step back. He was living next door to me now? Why? How? "I'm sorry, what?" I finally asked when my brain could catch up to what was happening.

"I'm renting Max's apartment until I can get approved to buy the apartment from him. I think I'll buy these ones," he said as he grabbed a box and held it up. "They should work."

I didn't care about the lightbulbs anymore. I was more concerned about the three little words he'd just uttered that now had my entire body heating from their meaning. "What do you mean *buy the apartment?*"

Jake shifted his stance, and I could tell that he was nervous. Good. He needed to feel that way. Not only was I going to be living next to him—possibly indefinitely.

Perhaps I needed to throw the apartment into the mix when I propose my offer.

"I'm not leaving Magnolia again," he finally said as he raised his gaze and offered me a soft smile. "I'm here to put down roots."

I furrowed my brow. "Roots?" Since when did Jake talk like this? He was a boat man. He hated staying on land for too long.

Jake crossed his arms over his chest, causing the box in his hand to stand straight up. "Yes. Roots. Is that hard to believe?"

I scoffed and nodded. "Um, yeah. You have *literally* never talked like this before. You love the ocean. Why are you giving that up?" My thoughts were traveling at a mile a minute and I was struggling to keep up with everything.

Jake studied me for a moment before he scoffed and passed by me. I followed behind him as he stepped up to the counter and set the lightbulbs down. "Would you believe me if I said people change?"

I moved to stand behind the register. My gaze met his, and for a moment, from the intensity of his stare, I wanted to believe it. That he could change. But I doubted it. "Not you," I said softly.

When Jake didn't respond, I glanced up at him to see that he had dropped his gaze to the counter. Guilt clung to my chest as I realized the weight of my words. I hadn't meant to hurt him, but that didn't matter, they had.

"I'm sorry," I said as I rang up his purchase. "Six forty-nine."

Jake nodded and handed me a ten. I retrieved his change from the drawer and placed it into his outstretched hand. We stood there for a moment, not speaking. It felt strange, and I wanted to say something—anything—to lessen the tension between us, but no words came to mind.

"Bag?" I asked as I turned to grab one.

"Naw. I'm not going far."

"Right." I turned back to him to see that he was watching me. I offered him a small smile. I wasn't sure what to do. I'd finished the transaction, which meant he was free to go. But he didn't seem like he was in any hurry. If anything, he looked as if he wanted to say something to me. And that made me nervous.

"Listen, Clem…" He wrinkled his nose as if he'd suddenly decided that the path he was headed down was the wrong one. He hesitated and then shook his head. "I'm sorry for the way I left things, and you have every right to hate me." He looked up and gave me his half smile that still weakened my knees. "I just hope that I can make it up to you somehow."

I chewed my lip. His words caused emotions to build up inside of me. I wasn't sure what they meant, and I wasn't sure if I even wanted to try to unpack them. Deciding that I didn't have the mental fortitude or clarity to attempt to discuss our past, I just nodded. "I look forward to that."

I cringed at my response, but there was no way I could take it back now. I'd said what I'd said, and the best thing I could do was end this conversation and wait until he left. So I offered him a weak smile and sighed. "I should get back to organizing the...nails." I blinked a few times, embarrassed by my own words. Jake paused before he nodded. "Right. Nails." He grabbed his lightbulbs. "I'll let you get back to your nails."

I shrugged and watched as he turned and made his way out of the store. Once the door shut behind him, I let out my breath. That was not at all how I'd seen this day going. It had gone from awful, to exciting, to awful again. My nerves were so rattled that I wasn't sure what to say or do anymore.

Sighing, I rubbed my temples and headed to the back room to make myself some coffee.

If I was going to have any chance of surviving the rest of the week—heck, the rest of the day—I needed as much caffeine as possible.

Stat.

SHARI

School was uneventful. Well, at least when I compared it to my home life, it felt uneventful. The kids were kids. Teachers were teachers. As chaotic as working at a school can be, it was normal. And right now, I was begging for normal.

The kids and I piled into the car, and as soon as we got home, they dropped their backpacks on the ground and Bella sprang to the living room while Tag ran to his bedroom. I was too tired to fight them, so I left them to their electronic devices as I headed into the kitchen to get started on dinner.

While the water was boiling for the noodles, I grabbed out my phone. My first thought was to text Craig to see if he was planning on coming home, but then I shook my head. He wasn't into returning my texts lately, and honestly, I wasn't even sure if I wanted him to come home.

Life was hard without him here—but it was equally as taxing when he was.

Not wanting to be alone, I swiped my phone on and pressed on Jake's name.

Me: Wanna come for dinner? We're having spaghetti.

I sent the text off and then proceed to pull out the bag of meatballs in the freezer. Once I popped them into the oven, I checked my phone for a response.

Jake: Hmmm. Garlic bread?

I chuckled as I replied with a *duh* and an emoji of a woman smacking her forehead.

Before I had time to put my phone down, his response came.

Jake: Yeah. I'll be there in thirty

I smiled as I set my phone down. I pulled out the French bread and sliced it in half. After buttering both sides, I sprinkled them with garlic salt and set them next to the stove. I'd slip them into the oven as soon as the meatballs came out.

Ten minutes later, the kitchen smelled of garlic and marinara. It made my mouth water. It must have also called to my children because soon Tag and Bella were sitting at the kitchen counter, watching me.

"Hungry?" I asked as I drained the pasta and tossed it with the sauce.

Bella nodded. "I'm starving." In true Bella fashion, she dragged out every sound in the word *starving*.

I dumped the meatballs in the leftover sauce and

moved to carry both bowls over to the table. "Well, wash up, it's almost ready."

Bella and Tag slipped off their chairs and disappeared. I headed back into the kitchen to slip the bread under the broiler. Just as I did, the back door opened.

"You're early," I said over my shoulder, not bothering to turn around.

"Who's early?"

Craig's voice startled me, causing me to slam the oven door on my fingers. I yelped and pulled them out. Out of instinct, I shoved them into my mouth to lessen the sting. I furrowed my brow when I met his narrowed eyes and clenched jaw muscles.

He was...angry. Why was he angry?

"I asked you, who's early?" He took a step forward and set two pizza boxes down on the counter.

I'd been too focused on his anger to process fully that he had brought home food. "What?" I asked, still not catching up on what was happening.

Craig growled and jabbed his finger toward the fourth plate I'd set. "Who's that for? I'm guessing it's not me."

I blinked a few times as my brain finally caught up to what he was saying. "I didn't know when you were going to get home. It's not like you answer me when I ask you." I walked over to the sink and washed my hands. I kept the water cool because, with the way I was feeling right now, I needed the temperature shock to keep a level head.

"Excuse me?" The tone of Craig's voice and his close proximity sent shivers down my spine. I swallowed and turned to see him towering over me. "I was getting us dinner, if you didn't notice."

I flicked off the water and grabbed a hand towel. I studied him as intently as he studied me. There was no way I was going to let on that he had rattled me. I needed to stand my ground.

"How was I supposed to know? It's not like you messaged me." I moved to grab the garlic bread out from under the broiler before it burned. I set the cookie sheet down on the stove and pulled off the oven mitt.

Craig hadn't moved. He remained rooted to the spot with his arms folded across his chest. "So who did you invite to dinner?" The accusatory tone in his voice made me scoff. He was joking, right?

"Who do you think? Jake." I stared at him like he was from a different world. "Did you think I was dating someone?" I threw up my hands and marched over to the fridge, where I pulled out a bottle of wine. I needed something to calm my nerves, especially if Craig was going to insist on being home.

"Well, you've haven't been talking to me, and when was the last time we had sex?" He spat the last words like I was the reason our sex life was non-existent.

"Shh," I said as I glared at him. I glanced around and leaned closer to the bathroom. It didn't sound like Tag or Bella were on their way back, so I straightened and moved to grab a wine glass. "That has nothing to do with me and everything to do with the fact that you run out of this house as fast as you can." I took a sip of my wine and studied him from over the rim of the glass.

Craig growled as he glared at me. "I'm working to provide. What the hell, Shari." He turned to plant his hands down on the counter and tip his head forward.

For a moment, I felt bad that we were fighting. I wasn't acting like I was so determined to make our marriage work. I wasn't doing everything I could to keep our relationship intact. Maybe I was assuming things when I didn't really know.

"I'm sorry," I said softly as I moved closer to Craig. Maybe if he would just open up to me, we could actually move forward like we needed to. I hesitated before I extended my hand and rested it on his forearm.

He flinched, but didn't pull away. Instead, he turned to study me. Then he sighed and straightened, breaking my connection with him. "I'm just stressed. It's not helpful when I come home to relax and Jake is here." Before I could do anything, he reached out and pulled me into a crushing hug.

I wanted to respond to what he said about Jake. Our issues started before Jake showed up, and it did bother me that his only reaction to our disintegrating marriage was to blame it on my brother.

But the longer I stood there, the more I began to realize that this might not be the time or place to address what he'd said. After all, Craig was sensitive about my family. I knew that. He struggled when they were around.

Attacking him about that now wasn't going to do anything to solve our issues.

It would only widen the chasm between us.

"Eww," Tag said as he came into the room and headed over to the table.

I pulled away from Craig, who was chuckling. "What do you mean?" he asked as he reached out and wrapped his arm around my shoulder and pulled me next to him. "Does this gross you out?"

Suddenly, Craig's lips were on mine. I was so startled that I almost pulled back and smacked him. But then my brain caught up and I reminded myself that this was my husband, not a stranger. It would be weird for me to react that way—even if it had been so long since we'd kissed that it *did* startle me.

Thankfully, it didn't last long. Craig pulled back and clapped his hands as he walked over to the pizza boxes and declared that they were what we were eating while watching a movie. I parted my lips to protest but then stopped myself. What harm would come from breaking the rules once in a while?

After all, Craig was home. Craig was involved. I should be grateful for that. Right now, that mattered more than the fact that I'd spent the last hour cooking dinner only to package it up for tomorrow.

It hurt, deep down in my stomach, but I decided not to dwell on it. Food was food. At least tomorrow I didn't have to worry about cooking. Everything was already done.

Just as I was wrapping the garlic bread up in tinfoil, the back door opened and Jake appeared. He was carrying a carton of ice cream, and when he saw me, his smile widened.

"Sorry I'm late," he said as he walked past me and over to the freezer. "Had to get ice cream."

I was rooted to the spot as I watched him. He straightened and turned, giving me a once-over.

"Eat a lemon?" he asked as he blew into his cupped hands and then rubbed them together.

I shook my head. "No." Then I took in a deep breath. I hated the fact that I'd invited my brother over only to tell him that he needed to leave. But he *did* need to leave. Craig was in a good mood, and I was going to capitalize on that for as long as I could.

Jake glanced around and then back to me, furrowing his brow. "Where's dinner? Did you eat it all?" The joking tone in his voice and the way he dramatically dropped his jaw just made me feel worse for what I was about to say.

"Craig's home," I said quietly. My cheeks burned. I knew how he felt about Craig, just like I knew how Craig felt about him. I hated being in the middle of their rift, but what could I do?

Craig was my husband. I had to stand by him. If not for my marriage's sake, for the sake of my kids. I needed to do what I could to keep my family intact.

"Ah," Jake said as he glanced toward the living room, where the sound of the newest Marvel movie was starting up, "Craig."

I winced. I hated that Craig didn't respect my views on which movies were appropriate for our children to watch. I wanted to intervene, but I kept chanting to myself that he was here and he was present. I couldn't complain if he was trying to make an effort.

"Yeah. He's finally off of work and got pizza for the kids to eat." I offered Jake an apologetic smile. Jake didn't look like he was going to take the bait. Instead, I sensed what he wanted to say, and every part of my being fought against hearing those words.

I didn't need to know that Craig was being a jerk right now. I didn't need Jake to tell me that we deserved better than what Craig was doing. I knew all of this. I just didn't know what to do about it.

How could I look my children in the eye later on and tell them that I truly did all that I could to make things work. Tag and Bella deserved a mom who at least tried. I wasn't ready to walk away just yet. I wasn't ready to give up.

"It's a start," I said slowly, hoping that Jake would pick up on the tone of my voice.

Jake glanced back at me, and I could see the irritation in his gaze. "He shouldn't have to *start* anything. He's your husband and those kids' father. It's his—"

"Jake." My patience snapped. I wasn't going to stand here and listen to Jake talk bad about Craig or try to tell me what I should or shouldn't be doing to make our marriage better. This was my life. This was my marriage. I was going to be the one to act, not Jake. This was an area where I wasn't interested in his input.

Jake's eyes widened as he stared at me. Then he let out his breath in a short manner that told me he wasn't happy with the way I'd snapped back at him. But he had to know that I was so close to breaking. One tap and I'd crumble to the ground.

Right now, I needed his support not his critique.

"I know how you feel about Craig, but now is not the time to bring that up," I said as I attempted to soften my tone with him. In my attempt to protect myself, I had to make sure I didn't alienate the only family I had. I may be irritated with Jake's insistence to enter into my life, but if I pushed too hard, he'd leave.

He'd already proven he had no problem doing that.

"I'm sorry," I whispered. I glanced up at him with pleading in my gaze, hoping he would understand.

Jake studied me for a moment before he sighed and ran his hand through his hair. "I should get going, big sis," he said as he reached out and pulled me into a hug. I patted his back as we stood there. He kissed me on the head and pulled back. "Call me if you need anything. I'm here."

I nodded and followed him outside. I walked him to his car, feeling a little lighter than I'd started the day out feeling.

"How's the business proposal going?" I asked as Jake unlocked his car.

"Good. Working on it now. I had to finish moving in

first." His voice drifted off as if he'd suddenly gotten distracted.

"Something happen with Clem?" I know when he got nostalgic, he was thinking of Clementine. And now that they were living next door to each other, meeting was going to be inevitable.

Jake scoffed and fiddled with his keys, which told me, yes, he'd had a run-in with her.

I shook my head. "You be careful with her. She's not as strong as she comes off being. After she put her dad in a home, I thought she was going to break." I raised my finger and shook it in his direction. "If you have no interest in starting things up again, walk away now. Leave her alone."

Jake was watching my finger, and then he grabbed my hand, halting my movement. "I get it," he said, his voice filled with more emotion than I'd expected.

It caused me to pause and watch my brother as he sighed and let go of my hand. He was conflicted, I could see it. Which could mean only one thing—he *wanted* to start things back up again with Clementine.

"Jake, what are you doing?" I asked. I loved my brother. I loved my best friend. I wanted nothing more than for them to be together. But I didn't trust that my brother wasn't going to leave again. He had a wandering spirit, and I wasn't sure it was something that he could so easily get rid of.

Jake kept his focus on the ground as he nodded a few times. "I know. I know." He sighed and scrubbed his face as he turned his gaze up to the sky. "I just can't continue leaving things the way I did." He shrugged. "I won't hurt her, I promise."

I studied him and then reached out and patted his upper arm. "I know you would never intentionally hurt her, but that doesn't mean that you couldn't do something that might bring up old feelings. Just, tread lightly."

Jake nodded and offered me a small smile. "I will." Then he reached out and tousled my hair. "You're such a good big sister," he said in a little kid voice.

I swatted his hand away and stepped out of his reach. "Hey, watch how you classify me." I narrowed my eyes at him. Having two babies wrecked havoc on my once petite figure.

"Aw, you know what I mean." He gave me a wink as he pulled open his truck door and slipped inside. He started the engine and then rolled the window down. "Seriously, though, call me if you need me. I can be here in five."

I pretended to stand at attention and salute him. He waved me away as he pulled out of the driveway and gave me a resounding *honk* as he turned and disappeared down the road. Now alone, I wrapped my arms around my chest and stared up at the sky, taking in the stars and moon, Jake's words still echoing in my mind.

I wanted to be able to tell him with a resounding *no* that I wasn't going to need his help—and that was still a hope I was holding onto. But deep down inside of me— really deep down—that hope was slowly burning down to embers.

At some point, the fire was going to be sufficiently put out that I would need to walk away. I just wasn't there yet. And the more I fought that reality, the more I began to understand my hesitation.

I was scared. I'd been married most of my adult life. My marriage and my family wasn't supposed to change. This wasn't the path I picked when I walked down the aisle and stood in front of Craig and declared my love for him.

I rubbed my upper arms as I headed back into the house and shut the back door behind me.

I needed to stop thinking like this. I needed to focus on the positive before the negative ate me alive. If my marriage was going to have even the slightest chance, I needed to recommit.

My children needed me to give it my all. Only then could I walk away. Only then would I quit.

10

CLEMENTINE

"Well, I think that is all we have to discuss." Kevin, the loan officer at Magnolia Bank, picked up the stack of papers I had just handed to him and tapped them on his desk. He then clipped them together and stuck them inside of a folder that he'd just prepared for me.

That folder held my future. All of that information was going to be used to discuss whether or not I was eligible for a loan. A loan for the building next door to mine. The building I was going to use to finally do something *I* wanted to do.

My dance studio.

My hands shook as I met Kevin's outstretched hand. We shook, and he rounded his desk and led me out of his office.

"I should have more information for you by the end of the week. But everything looks good. I'm sure it will be good news." We stood in the lobby now, and my entire body felt as if it were going to collapse. Partly because of the fear I felt, embarking on this journey all by myself. But mostly because I was scared that I would fail. That everything would line up for me, and I would somehow destroy my one chance at doing what I wanted to do.

What I was born to do.

"Thanks, Kevin. I look forward to hearing from you." I offered him a smile, hoping it covered up the nerves I felt. We said our goodbyes and I headed to the exit. Just as I went to push open the door, it swung open, startling me.

I glanced up to see Jake standing there with a surprised expression.

"Hey, Clem," he said. It was so smooth and relaxed that it took me right back to our dating years where he would say my name and then gather me up into his arms and hold me.

The fact that I actually longed for his arms to surround me startled me in a way that I didn't like. Muscle memory was real. Just two words from him and my entire body reacted. It made me angry at myself. How could I protect my heart if I longed for him every time I heard him say my name or saw his face.

It wasn't fair.

"Jake," I said quickly as I moved past him and outside. The weather had warmed, and I reveled in the feeling of the sun beating down on my face. I hoped I'd be able to leave before he caught up with me, but I was wrong. Just as I slipped into the driver's seat, Jake's hand caught my door and made it impossible for me to shut it.

I glanced up to see him peering down at me with a smile. My stomach jolted and my heart began to race. I swallowed hard, hoping that would remove this feeling from my body, and said, "What's up?"

Jake stood there in a sort of daze. His gaze moved to his hand and he quickly pulled it back. "I'm sorry. I didn't mean to grab your door. I was just..." His voice drifted off and he pinched his lips together as if he didn't want to finish his sentence.

But I wasn't going to let him off that easy. "You were just?"

He scrubbed his face and then glanced back at me. "I was just worried that you were going to run off if I tried to talk to you."

Butterflies were now assaulting my stomach, and I took in a deep breath, trying to calm the feelings inside of me. "What did you need to talk to me about?" Why was I so anxious? It probably had nothing to do with our previous relationship and was something mundane—like, I needed to be better at parking behind the store because I was crowding him out.

Thankfully, he didn't leave me in suspense for too long. His expression turned stoic, and I found myself straightening in my seat. I knew Jake. He wasn't Mr. Serious. If things got hard, he just left.

I was proof of that.

"Can we go somewhere for lunch?" he finally asked.

I blinked a few times. This was what he was so scared to talk to me about? Inviting me to lunch? "Um…" I cleared my throat. "Right now?"

Jake squinted as he studied me and then dropped his gaze. "Yeah. I, um, need to discuss something with you."

I stared at him, too scared to say yes, but equally as scared to say no. "Okay." My response was a whisper and caused Jake to lean closer. "Okay," I said, this time louder.

Jake smiled and pulled his keys from his pocket. "Perfect. I'll meet you at the Eatery?"

I personally wanted some greasy fries from Shakes, but with the way my jeans were fitting lately, I could probably use something lighter and healthier. So I nodded, shut my door, and started up my engine.

The entire drive over to the Eatery, I wanted to make a left turn and drive as far and as fast as I could away from Jake. I wasn't sure what he wanted to talk about, but I was fairly certain I wasn't going to like it. At least, I wasn't going to leave without some sort to scarring.

I pulled into the parking spot next to the one Jake had pulled into and turned off my engine. I stepped out of my car only to find Jake waiting for me by his bumper. He smiled at me, and warning bells sounded in my mind. Why was he smiling at me? What was this about?

I cleared my throat to ground myself and to snap myself out of the internal freak-out I seemed to be experiencing right now. This was just lunch. That was all. He wasn't proclaiming his love to me or telling me that he wanted to get back together again.

It was just two once-friends who were going to try to attempt reconciliation through a shared meal. That was all.

That was *all*.

But no matter how many times I chanted that in my mind, the blasted butterflies didn't take notice. Instead, when Jake held open the door for me, they decided it would best to dive-bomb my stomach instead of calming down to a manageable flutter.

We were seated within a few minutes with menus in both of our hands. I decided on a house salad with their fresh baked bread, and Jake ordered a Reuben with fries. We handed our menus back to our waitress, and silence engulfed our table.

I sat there, fiddling with my straw, trying to figure out why Jake wasn't talking. He seemed so desperate earlier, but now that he had my undivided attention, he was clamming up. I felt a tad whiplashed from this entire experience.

"So…" I raised my eyebrows. "What's up?"

Jake took a sip of his milkshake and set it down. He then entwined his fingers and set them on the table. "I, um, wanted to talk to you about something personal."

My eyebrows rose higher. "Personal?"

He nodded. "There's not many people I can talk to about this. At least, not that I would trust with this information."

My heart was pounding now. "Okay," I said slowly. I

had no idea where this conversation was going, and that uncertainty scared me.

Jake sighed and then paused, his silence killing me. Finally he took in a deep breath and said, "I'm worried about Shari."

It took a second for my brain to catch up with his words. I hadn't expected him to say that, and so all of my preparation wasn't going to help me now.

"Shari?" I asked after I took a sip of my Diet Coke.

He nodded. "Things are weird at her place, and I keep trying to talk to her about it, but she's shutting me out. Which only tells me that things are a *lot* worse than I originally thought."

I studied the tabletop as I thought on what he'd said. He wasn't lying. I felt it too. Shari was pulling away from me. She was going through something, and I had a feeling it had everything to do with Craig and nothing to do with her. She was protecting him for some reason, and I couldn't quite pinpoint why.

Our food was delivered, and I waited for the waitress to leave before speaking. "I know what you mean. Things have been getting worse for a while now. Shari is left to carry the bulk of the work with the kids and the house. Craig is always gone." I shook my head as my emotions began to build in my throat. I hadn't realized until now—as I spoke the words out loud—just how worried I was about my friend.

Shari had a way of making everyone feel comfortable even if it was to the detriment of her own happiness. She never wanted people to stress for her sake, but when I stepped back and really analyzed my friend, it made me realize that I'd been failing her.

She was hurting, and I'd done nothing to help ease that burden.

"Craig is always gone?" Jake asked as he munched on a fry.

I nodded.

"Hmm. So that means he wasn't leaving because I was there." He tapped his fingers on the table—a telling sign that he was deep in thought.

"Things still rough between you two?" I speared a tomato and slipped it into my mouth. It was no secret that Craig hated the Palmers even though he married into the family. It broke her family's heart, but Shari had gotten good at playing referee between them—maybe it was the practice she got from their messy divorce. It made me feel for my friend, but there wasn't much I could do besides be supportive.

"Well, they were getting that way, which is why I moved into Max's place. I want to give Shari her space while still being around to help out."

I chewed on my bite of bread as I thought about his words. He wanted to stick around. That was the first time I'd ever heard him express this much interest in Magnolia.

"So you're really sticking around for good?" I needed to know his answer to this question. If I was going to allow myself to get even slightly emotionally invested in Jake, I needed to know that it wasn't going to be in vain.

That he was going to stay in Magnolia. If we were going to help Shari together, then he needed to hold up his end of that bargain.

Jake studied me for a moment before he nodded. "Yeah. I'm done with being on a boat. It was nice while it lasted, but I began to realize that there was a lot about land that I missed." His gaze met mine, and my stomach flipped inside of my body.

Was he talking about me? Or Shari? I allowed myself to hope—for a moment—that he meant me. But then I pushed that ridiculous thought from my mind and turned my energy to focus on Shari and how we were going to help solve this issue.

"Yeah. I bet it was a shock to see how big Bella and Tag got." My cheeks were burning from the intensity of his stare as he kept his focus on me. I took a long drink of my soda, hoping it would help cool my body down. Why was I reacting this way? I was a fool to think that we could just pick up where we left off or that Jake even wanted that.

I was sure he was just being nice, that was all.

He was nice.

Period.

"It was a shock. Especially Tag. That kid is moody."

I chuckled. "Yeah, he's definitely in pre-teen mode."

Jake nodded. "He needs a swift kick in the pants."

"And you have room to talk? Should we go through the list of teenage rebellions you went through? Remember the trouble we used to get into?" The words were out of my mouth before I could stop them. I hadn't meant to bring up our history. There was too much pain associated with that, and for me to just mention it so nonchalantly was foolish.

What was he supposed to do with that? What was I?

I peeked up at Jake to see that his expression had softened. It was almost as if he were enjoying the memories. Which seemed strange to me. I'd always assumed that he hated Magnolia and everything that came with it. Hence his uncontrollable desire to leave it.

But the way he was smiling and the far-off look in his eye told me that perhaps I was wrong. Perhaps, there was something more that I didn't understand.

"Yeah, I was a hooligan." He took a big bite of his sandwich and swallowed before speaking again. "Good thing I finally grew up."

I quirked an eyebrow. "But have you?"

He studied me for a moment before he shrugged. "I'd like to think I have."

I sat back and watched him dip some of his fries into ketchup and then slip them into his mouth. He looked older, that was for sure. But not in a bad way. He had some grey hair in the beard he'd allowed to grow scruffy around his face. His dark hair was longer than how he'd kept it when he was younger. The edges of his hair curled in way that made my fingers ache to run through them.

I swallowed as the desire to feel his arms around me once more washed over me. I knew how it felt. I know how at home I felt when I was pressed against his chest, listening to his heartbeat. I knew how he completed me in more ways than one.

And I would be lying to myself if I didn't admit that I missed it. It was a deep down, soul-crushing ache. One that caused my heart to pound and my body to lighten when I thought about it.

And it made me angry that I still felt this way. Especially when it was pretty obvious that our future had ended the day he boarded the bus to take him as far away from Magnolia as possible.

Needing to shift my focus onto something that wasn't memories of Jake, I took a sip of my soda and folded my hands in my lap. "So what do we do?" I asked.

Jake furrowed his brow, wiped his fingers on a nearby napkin, and then took what sounded like the final sips of his shake.

"About Shari," I added, just in case he couldn't follow my shift in conversation.

He nodded. "I was hoping that we could put our heads together to help her." He closed his eyes and rubbed his temples. I watched as stress overtook his expression. I could tell that he was worried about Shari—as was I—but it was also a struggle for me to see him hurting.

"Yeah," I said softly. I understood his plight. Truth was, I'd felt the same for a while now. I wanted to help; I just didn't know how.

"I think it's best if we come at this together in a non-threatening way. She can't feel like we are ganging up on her and talking bad about Craig—"

"Or she'll just run to him," Jake said, finishing my statement. He furrowed his brow, and I paused because I could tell that he was fighting with something internally. "What do you think is going on?" he finally asked. He studied me as if he knew I had the answer.

But I didn't. I had suspicions, but that was all. Shari's lips were tighter than a ship about this. And I didn't want her to think that I was gossiping about her. But when it was her brother asking the questions, it really wasn't gossip. We both cared for her enough to want to help.

"I'm not sure. I have my suspicions, but that's it."

Jake furrowed his brow as he tapped his fingers on the table. "Do you think he's cheating?" he asked as he lowered his voice and leaned in.

I chewed my lip and then slowly nodded. Jake leaned back, folding his arms over his chest. I heard him swear quietly under his breath, but I didn't say anything. I had the same exact sentiments.

"So how do we help?"

I speared the last of my salad and chewed thoughtfully. Then I leaned forward. "What if we threw you, like, a party? Then we could talk to her in an unthreatening way afterward and see if she'll open up to us."

Jake's half smile emerged, and I could see the flirtation in his gaze. My cheeks flushed and I couldn't help but smile as well. Jake's grins had the same effect on people as yawns. Once you saw him do it, you couldn't help but do it yourself.

I used all the facial muscle strength I had to pull my

lips back down. I didn't want him to know the kind of reaction he inspired in me. But it was too late.

"You want to throw me a party?" he asked in his teasing voice.

I glowered at him. "It's only for research purposes. A front, one could say."

Jake nodded, but the look on his face said *yeah right*.

"Okay." He raised his hands. "I guess I have to let you throw me a party."

I sighed, realizing that I'd walked right into that one. Even though it wasn't what I wanted to do, I was a little excited to be busy with something more than working at the store or dreaming about my life changing.

I had to wait for the bank to respond to me, so I might fill that time with other things. I leaned back in my seat and watched Jake finished his food. It wasn't until I was back at the store and relieving Michelle, that realization hit me.

I had just offered to throw a homecoming party for Jake Palmer.

What had I done?

SHARI

Thank goodness it was Friday. The week had moved by like a snail. When the final bell rang at school, I helped get the kids out of the hallway, and then Bella, Tag, and I said goodbye to Cassidy, climbed into the car, and headed home.

It was a beautiful afternoon. The sun was shining, and the air smelled like summer. The salty breeze hit my senses, and the memories of my adolescent time at the beach washed over me. Back then all my worries consisted of what bikini I was going to wear or which boy liked me.

It was a simpler time, even though back then I hadn't felt that way. I'd been convinced my world was going to end if anything embarrassing happened. Or if the guy of the hour didn't smile at me.

Little did I know, adulthood held the same disappointments.

After our family dinner on Monday, Craig slipped back into old habits. He spent more time away from the house than he did in it. His conversations with me were short and curt. Whatever had happened to change his mind on Monday must have worn off because we were right back to where we'd fallen. Distant and alone.

I'd managed to avoid Jake like Craig avoided me. Finally, last night, he came over and said he was taking the kids to the arcade to give me the night off. It was amazing. I ordered Chinese, took a bath, and binge-watched a K-drama that Clementine had got me hooked on.

It was heaven, and I was grateful that Jake had helped me out—even though I'd been mean to him. When he brought the kids home and helped me put them to bed, he stuck around for a few minutes, letting me know about a homecoming party that Clementine had planned for him.

I was shocked to hear that Clementine wanted anything to do with Jake, but when I texted her later, she said she was offering an olive branch. With the way Craig felt about Jake, the last thing I needed was for my best friend to hate him too, so I decided to look at this like my life just got a tad easier.

A truce was better than a battle. I was already facing so many battles on my own that I didn't want to impede the process of one resolving on its own.

So this morning, when Clementine texted and asked me if I wanted to help her plan the party, I agreed. After all, I wasn't going on any sexy date tonight. Margaritas and Pinterest sounded like a good time to me.

I settled the kids down with a to-go pizza and a movie right at five. The doorbell rang three minutes after that, just as I pulled the ice from the freezer.

"Come in," I called toward the door.

But Clementine hadn't waited for my response and was already heading into the kitchen as the last word left my lips. I laughed as I shook my head. "Why do you even ring the doorbell?"

She set the bag from El Azteca, the local Mexican restaurant, down on the island and began to pull out the to-die-for salsa and chips.

I grabbed the limes and margarita mix from the fridge, and in a few short moments, we had ourselves some ice-cold, frothy drinks. With our food and liquid courage in hand, we made our way into the dining room and sat down.

It wasn't until half the chips were gone that we spoke. I enjoyed the stinging sensation on my lips from the spice of the salsa. Craig hated anything spicy. He complained that he wanted to taste his food, not have it burn off his taste buds. So we always went mild where he was concerned.

But Clementine was like me. She didn't fear a little heat. So we devoured the chips and salsa like a zombie apocalypse was knocking at our door and this was the last time we were going to eat.

When our lips were sufficiently numb and the margaritas were melting, I turned my attention to Clementine.

"So, should I address the elephant in the room?" I asked as I raised my eyebrows.

She busied herself with wiping some chip crumbs off the table and scooping them into her hand. After she tossed them in the garbage, she came back with her brows furrowed.

"Elephant? What elephant?" she asked as she sat down at the table.

"Um, the giant elephant of *you want to throw my brother a homecoming party?*" I shook my head. Something was up. I could feel it. Clementine had never been a good liar.

Ever.

She sighed and tipped her head back, closing her eyes for a moment. Then she glanced over at me and shrugged. "We're neighbors now, so I figured we should at least attempt to get along. Is that so bad?"

I scoffed and swirled the last drink of margarita around in my glass. "Not bad, just…strange." I glanced over at her. "Are you sure that's all?"

She pinched her lips together as she swiped on her iPad. Then she glanced over at me sheepishly. "You're right. There's something more."

I knew it.

"Show me."

She got shy for a moment, pulling the iPad close to her chest before bringing it down and laying it in front of me. *In Motion Dance Studio* was written across the top of a Word document.

"In Motion?" I asked, glancing over at her to see if I'd read that right.

Clementine nodded. "This is the dance studio I want to start. It'll be perfect. Right next door to the store." She sighed, and her eyes got a far-off look to them as she sat back. "I'm finally going to be doing what I want."

I stared at her, trying to process what she was saying. I was happy for her. After all, she'd given up all of her dreams to stay in Magnolia to take care of her father. I couldn't think of anyone more deserving of this than her. But I had a lot of concerns. Clementine had a tendency to jump feet first into things, and the results, for the most part, were disastrous.

Without her parents around, I feared that she might unwittingly give away her one source of income for a dream that might not come to fruition. "Really? That's exciting," I said. I didn't want to crush her dreams, and I knew that I was going to need to tread lightly if I was going to have any ability to guide her.

Clementine chewed her lip. "I know. I'm so nervous I'm sick." She wrapped her arm around her waist and leaned forward. "Waiting to hear back from the bank is killing me," she whispered.

I reached out and patted her hand. "I'm sure it will go well," I said, offering her a smile.

Clementine took in a deep breath. "I hope so." Then she scrolled down on her screen and tipped the iPad so I could see it. "Wanna see the plans I have for the space?"

"Space?"

She nodded. "Max's hobby shop. He's waiting for me to put in my bid before he makes a decision on who he is going to sell it to."

"Max's shop?"

Clementine nodded. "Yeah. He's retiring and looking for someone to take over. He said he already had someone interested, but he's waiting until I can get my quote back from the bank before he decides." Clementine picked up a chip and turned it around between her fingers.

She got a far-off look in her eyes, and I couldn't help but feel happy for her, but at the same time I felt worried. Things were moving faster for her than I liked, but I also didn't want to be the one to crush her dreams. I just wished she'd take her time thinking this through before she just jumped in.

Once she got financially involved, there wouldn't be much she could do to get out if she decided it was a bad idea. And the last thing I wanted was to see my best friend struggle.

We spent the rest of the night planning the BBQ we were going to host the next day. Clementine said she already got Maggie's permission to host it at the inn in the backyard by their newly created fire pit. I thought that would be the perfect way to spend a Saturday evening.

We also decided on an Evite to send to the members of the town that knew and loved Jake. Our list ended up being about fifty people. We wanted to keep it small but eventful. And any exposure we could give to Maggie and the inn was good exposure. She was struggling ever since her soft launch, and I felt a moral obligation to help her out.

We all did.

Clementine left around ten, and I moved into the living room to carry Bella off to bed. Tag was still awake, and he moved when I asked him to—which was a first for him. Lately, anything I said, he tried to counter with a grumble and sigh. I was grateful that I didn't have to fight him to go to bed tonight.

I was too tired to deal with that.

Once I rinsed out our dishes and turned off all the lights, I headed into my room, where I shut the door and crawled under my covers. The screen from my phone lit up the room as I spent the next thirty minutes scrolling through all the social media platforms. My eyes grew heavy, and just as I allowed them to fall closed, the bedroom door opened.

I shifted to sit, ready to take on whatever nightmare Bella had just had, but to my surprise, Craig entered the room. My entire body tensed as I watched him shut the door and then move to his closet while unbuttoning his shirt.

I hadn't expected him to come home, and I was confused why he was here. "No work tonight?" I asked as I rubbed the sleep from my eyes and sat up straighter.

Craig disappeared into his closet only to appear a few seconds later with his shirt fully unbuttoned and his white undershirt showing. "I got off early. I was caught up on all of my paperwork, so I told the boys I was coming home to spend time with my wife."

The words sounded so strange coming from his lips. I studied him with my brow furrowed. Since when did he call me his *wife*? Or speak about me in that way? Like he was desperate to see me or something.

"Oh," was the only response I could make. I wasn't sure what he meant by anything that he'd said, and I wasn't sure if I should even allow myself to hope that it meant our relationship might be turning around. That there was still a chance for us.

As those thoughts floated around, a dark cloud settled on my mind. I realized that I just might have to make a decision about my marriage sooner than I'd anticipated. With Craig distant, I could avoid the decision to stay or go. But with him home, staring at me, speaking to me in this way, it caused a fear in me that my future was going to be decided very soon. And that idea left me feeling panicked.

I wasn't sure I was ready for any of this.

Craig finished undressing and came into the room with just his boxers and undershirt on. He disappeared into the bathroom, and a few minutes later came back out and flopped onto the bed. It took him a few minutes to get situated, but when he finally stopped moving, I snuck a peek at him.

This was…strange. I didn't like it. There was too much unknown about him being home when I'd expected him to be gone, and that mystery was eating me alive.

"Did you have a good day?" he finally asked me.

I dropped my gaze to my hands when he tipped his head to the side to study me. Butterflies were assaulting my stomach and not in a good way. I was anxious, and there was no way that discussing mundane things was going to mitigate these reactions. But I didn't want to have the in-depth conversation we needed to have either, so I decided to just go along with it.

"School was good. The kids and I came back here and hung out until Clementine came over. She's planning a homecoming party for...Jake." I pinched my lips together. In my haste to fill the silence around us with conversation, I'd accidentally brought up my brother. And from the look on Craig's face—like he'd just ingested a lemon—this wasn't the conversation he wanted to have either.

But I'd already started, so I might as well finish. "It's going to be small and at the inn. We're hoping it will get more people visiting the inn, which should help Maggie."

Craig's expression remained stoic as he nodded along with my words. When I finished, he glanced over at me.

"When is the party?"

"Tomorrow night."

Craig's expression dropped. "Tomorrow?"

I nodded. "Why? Is there something else going on?" How could he get mad that I'd made plans? He was never home. I'd just figured he was going to be at work.

I braced myself for the backlash that always came when he felt I'd wronged him. But it never came. Instead, he stilled his expression and faced me. Almost as if he were attempting to calm his anger.

Which, even though it angered me that he felt he had a right to be frustrated with me for making plans without him, I was happy to see that his first reaction wasn't to lash out. I could get used to this.

"Well, I guess that's a good thing because I booked us a room at the inn tomorrow night as well."

I paused as I let his words settle around me. Did he say what I thought he said? "You did?" I asked, turning to face him.

Craig nodded. "I wanted to do something special for you and figured a night away would be the perfect answer. Carol is going to take the kids so we can go." He shrugged. "I mean, if that's okay with you."

I raised my eyebrows as I stared at him. It took a moment for me to respond as his words left me surprised and confused. "Um, yeah. Sure. That sounds amazing." I gave him a smile that for the first time, didn't feel forced. "You can be my plus-one to the party and then we can just head upstairs afterward."

He hesitated before he shook his head. "How about you go to the party and then meet me upstairs?" He offered me a weak smile. "You know how I am about parties."

I wasn't going to lie, his response hurt me. I wanted him to get used to doing things with me. And Jake…well he was a part of my life now, and from what he said, he wasn't going to be leaving.

The sooner my husband could get over his anger toward my brother, the better my life would be all around. But then I realized I couldn't demand this much change in such a short amount of time. If I wanted to better my marriage, then we needed to start with just us and work from there.

Craig said goodnight and kissed me on the cheek before he turned over and his snores filled the silence. I remained awake a bit longer, lying on my back and staring up at the darkness above me.

My mind was full of all sorts of questions, and I wasn't sure which to address—or if I even had the capacity to address any of them at the moment.

Regardless, this weekend was going to be the time when truths came out and decisions were made.

Was my marriage broken beyond repair? Or were we both under the impression that we wanted to fix what we'd built?

We'd find out tomorrow. No matter what.

12

CLEMENTINE

I was grateful that Michelle agreed to work all day today so that I could head over the bridge and pick up all the food items we were going to need for Jake's party. It wasn't so much about the party as it was what we were going to do afterward. I was ready to have it out with Shari, and knowing that Jake backed me up on my assumption helped.

I didn't want to be alone, and even though that meant I needed to conspire with Jake, I was willing to do it. I cared too much about my friend to let her suffer in silence any longer.

Nine rolled around, and I was showered and dressed. I decided to run some mousse through my hair and allow it to curl. I was wearing a white peasant top with dark, cut-off jean shorts. With my Converse's on, I was ready for a day of speed shopping.

Maggie was more than thrilled to allow us to throw this party at the inn, saying that we would have the run of the backyard grill and gazebo. She even said that she would get Archer to string the twinkle lights. I thanked her and told her I'd be there around five to prep the food.

I slung my purse over my shoulder and nodded at my reflection in the mirror. I had plenty of time to get everything done that I needed to.

The air was warm as I pushed through the back door and headed outside. I pulled my purse up and was digging through it to find my keys when Jake's voice stopped me in my tracks.

"I thought I saw your light go on this morning," he said. His voice had a teasing tone to it.

I slowly glanced up to see Jake leaning against my car with his legs extended out in front of him. He was wearing a dark blue t-shirt that accented his blue eyes and some khaki cargo shorts. His hair was damp as if he'd just gotten out of the shower, and his ridiculously sexy half smile was spread across his lips.

I blew out the breath that had caught in my throat as I narrowed my eyes at him. "Are you stalking me?"

He chuckled and shook his head. "Naw. Your window is across from mine," he said as he pointed up at my window.

My gaze followed his gesture and I nodded. "Right."

"Heading out?"

I nodded as I slipped my finger into my key ring and fiddled with the keys on it.

"Want company?"

I raised my gaze up to meet his. "You want to go grocery shopping with me?"

Jake studied my gaze for a moment before he nodded. "Yes. I need a few items that they don't provide on the island." He grasped his hands together in a begging manner. "You'd really be saving me, that's all."

I narrowed my eyes at him and contemplated saying no, but the help with carrying groceries was draw enough for me to sigh and nod. "Okay."

He straightened, and the fact that his grin deepened caused my heart to pound harder. "Want me to drive?"

Sitting in the passenger seat, relaxing while all the scenery passed by me, seemed like just what I needed to start my day. So I nodded and shoved my keys back into my purse as I followed him over to his truck.

We both climbed in, and soon, we were on the road. Jake was relaxing in the driver's seat with his wrist on the steering wheel and Jack Johnson blaring from his speakers. I chuckled, and Jake must have noticed because he glanced over at me with a wide grin.

"What?" he asked.

I shook my head. "Nothing."

"What?" he asked again.

I leaned back in my seat and crossed my legs, my arm resting on the joint armrest between us. "It's just that some things never change."

Jake scoffed and then flexed his arm. "I'd say that a lot of things have changed."

My gaze slipped down to his arm and the new muscles that existed there. Years of working on a fishing boat had done him good, I'd give him that. So much so that the physical part of me—the one part that I tried to ignore around him—responded to just looking at his arms.

The thought of what it might feel like to be wrapped in his arms once more caused my heart to begin to thrum in my ears.

I cleared my throat—hoping to dispel that sound—and turned to stare out the window again. "You're the Hulk," I murmured under my breath.

Jake laughed, and it sounded so carefree and open that it made my whole body ache. Why did things feel so easy with him? It was like all I needed was to hear his laughter and see him standing next to me for me to give up my anger for him. Why couldn't I hate him like I needed to?

I feared if I allowed myself to be around him, to let him back into my life, I was going to have a hard time keeping my feelings for him straight. It was pretty obvious that I hadn't gotten over him like I'd originally thought, and I didn't need my ability to fall for him once more to cloud my judgement.

"The Hulk," he whispered before he began to sing along with "*Home*."

I tried to relax until we got to the grocery store, but when Jake drove past it, my anxiety went up and I glanced over at him. "We were—"

"I want to stop by somewhere else first," he said as he glanced over at me and gave me a wink.

I pulled back slightly. I wasn't sure if it was his words or his wink, but either way, I couldn't stop my confusion at what he was doing from growing inside of me.

"Okay," I said slowly.

Jake reached over and patted my hand. My entire body warmed from his touch. "Don't worry, you will be fine," he said and returned his hand to the steering wheel.

I sat there, frozen. Jake had just touched me, and I'd responded to that touch. And now, he was moving on like nothing had happened while I was stuck here, trying to process how I felt about it. He looked as if nothing had happened; he was completely at ease.

It wasn't fair.

Jake pulled into the Jolly Time Arcade and turned off the engine. I stared, open-mouthed, at the weather-worn paint on the outside of the building. Such a stark contrast to the vivid paint from when it first opened, years ago.

I furrowed my brow as I unbuckled and glanced over at Jake, whose mischievous grin was growing wider by the second.

"Is it even open?" I asked as I pulled on the door handle and hopped down onto the asphalt.

Jake chuckled as he rounded the hood of his truck, threw his keys into the air, and then shoved them into his pocket. "It's a Saturday morning. Peak business hours."

I followed after him as he pulled open the black-tinted door and held it for me to enter. The smell of sweaty kids and popcorn filled my nose as I entered the building. The familiar dinging sound from the games surrounded me, and I couldn't stop the smile that formed on my lips.

It was like stepping back into my childhood, coming in here. Back in time to a place where I was happier and carefree. Where I still had both of my parents and my whole life was ahead of me. If only I had known then what I knew now.

"Ready for me to whip your butt?" Jake asked as he passed by me.

His words caught me off guard, and I turned to face him just as he paused and turned to face me. I stared at him with wide eyes and then we both busted out laughing.

"Er…Ready for me to beat you?" he asked as he stepped up to the nose-ring wearing cashier kid who was busily chewing his gum and playing some game on his phone.

I nodded. "I think what you mean is, are you ready for *me* to beat *you*." I said as I pressed my hand to my chest and then waved it toward him.

Jake snorted as the cashier placed the cup of coins onto the counter and then handed Jake's card back to him. After he slipped his wallet into his back pocket, Jake grabbed the tokens and turned to me, shaking them for emphasis.

"Let's do this thing," he said as he made a beeline for his favorite game, the one where the light moves around in a circle and you have to attempt to stop the light on a specific color.

"Of course you would pick that one," I said as I moved to stand next to him, our shoulders touching.

Jake laughed as he slipped the tokens into the game. "I've gotta start out with a bang. If I'm going to win the most tickets, I need to do what I'm good at."

I glanced over at the prize counter as the memories of coming here washed over me. We'd spent almost every summer day here when we were dating. The bet was whoever had the most tickets got the pot. We were saving up for a ridiculously overstuffed monkey. But things with Dad got worse, and I needed to help around the store more.

Eventually, we stopped coming, and I wasn't even sure what I'd done with the shoebox full of tickets.

"Your turn," Jake said as he happily produced a trail of tickets that went all the way down to the floor.

I narrowed my eyes at him as he carefully stacked the tickets onto each other. I grabbed the cup of tokens and headed over to Skee-ball, my all-time favorite game.

"Ooo, I like it," Jake said as he followed after me.

I shot him an annoyed look as I slipped a token into the slot. "No. No you don't. This is my game." I waved him away. He wasn't going to rain on my success.

Jake snorted and grabbed a token from the cup before I could pull it away. He laughed as he slipped the coin into the machine next to me and it whirred to life.

"I think you've just made this a competition," he said as he grabbed the first ball and threw it up the ramp.

"How can it be a competition if I wipe the floor with

you?" I asked as I slid the ball up the ramp and it soared into the 50 spot.

"Oh, big talk from an amateur," he said as his ball flew right into one of the 100 spots. He let out a cheer, and it only riled me up more.

I narrowed my eyes at the 100 spot and began sinking balls into the goal. I cheered at each score, and soon, Jake started cheering with me. When I ended my round, I'd officially gotten five 100-point scores. It was the most I'd ever done.

I gleefully laughed as the tickets began spitting out of the machine. I gathered them up and then stood, waving them in his face in a very unladylike manner. "I won," I said.

Jake laughed as he ripped his measly number of tickets from the machine. "You did." He straightened. "I guess all of my Skee-ball training in Anchorage was for nothing."

The words seemed so relaxed as he released them and they floated through the air, but my entire body paused as they reached my ears. Anchorage. He'd gone to Anchorage. To get away from me.

My cheeks heated from the memory of him walking away from me. My stomach clenched from the all too familiar feeling of abandonment. I had been so broken after he left, and yet here I was, willingly letting him back into my life.

"Are you okay?" Jake's furrowed brow entered my line of sight, and out of instinct, I pulled back and ducked my head down.

"I need a soda," I said as I headed to the door. Once outside, I made my way to the vending machines on the side of the building. They were filled with cans of off-brand soda that you can't help but like because of the strange taste they had. Thankfully, they hadn't changed the machines, and I fished around in my purse until I found fifty cents and slipped it into the slot.

The machine rumbled and the can of grape soda I'd just selected, thudded to the bottom. I grabbed it out and cracked it open, moving to the picnic table next to the machines.

Jake grabbed a soda and moved to sit down but paused. I could feel his stare on me as he stood there, as if he were wondering if it was okay that he join me.

"You can sit," I said softly, nodding toward the bench across from me.

Jake nodded and slipped onto the seat. The cracking sound from him opening his soda filled the silence. We sat there, sipping our drinks and not talking.

I sighed as I stared at the condensation on my can, drawing my finger through it and watching the moisture collect into droplets. My mind was racing with what had happened and my reaction. It bothered me that it still affected me—what he'd done. And I knew I was never going to move on until I addressed what had happened.

I couldn't pretend that what he'd done to me didn't still haunt me to this day. And if we were going to have any kind of relationship, it needed to be addressed.

"I'm sorry," he said. His voice was quiet and reserved.

When I glanced up to look at him and took in his downturned gaze and slumped shoulders, my heart began to pound. He knew why I'd reacted this way. He knew that he'd hurt me. And he felt bad.

This was a start.

"It's okay," I said out of instinct. What else was I supposed to say? I no longer wanted to berate him for what had happened. After all, years had passed since he left. But I needed him to know that he'd hurt me, and I wasn't sure if I could trust him with those feelings. I wanted to, but I knew my journey toward trusting him again was going to be a slow and strategic one.

"No, it's not okay." Jake reached out and ran his finger over the outside of his can, much like I'd done. I could tell that he was drawing some sort of design in the condensation. "Clem, I know this isn't going to make up for the pain I caused you or the trust I lost, but I am truly sorry for the way I treated you. I shouldn't have just left. Not like I did." His voice had deepened, and my entire body responded to his words.

My heart pounded, my breathing deepened, and tears clung to my lashes. I didn't realize it until now, but I needed to hear those words. I needed to hear that acknowledgment from him. I drummed my fingers on the tabletop a few times before I pinched my lips together and nodded.

"Why did you leave?" I asked through the emotions that had collected in my throat.

He furrowed his brow as he studied me. Then he took

a sip of his soda before he sighed and brought his gaze back up to meet mine. "I was scared."

"Scared?"

He nodded. "Scared of how I felt for you."

I was mid-sip, and I nearly spit all of the soda in my mouth onto him. I coughed as I set the can down so I could focus on what he'd said. My heart felt like a horse out for a run for the first time in years. Free and unrestrained.

"How you felt for me?"

Jake had dropped his gaze to the tabletop and seemed to be staring very intently at it. I watched him, unable to keep my gaze from his. He twisted the can around a few times before raising his gaze back up to meet mine.

"It wasn't until I walked away that I realized just how much I cared about you. And how much I missed you." He swallowed, and I could see his Adam's apple rise and fall. "But I'd already hurt you. I convinced myself that you would never forgive me, and I didn't want to put that burden on you. So I stayed away."

My hands were shaking now as I reached out to grab my soda and bring it to my lips. I reveled in the feeling of the cool soda as it washed over my throat. Then I set the can back down and returned my attention to Jake.

"You missed me?" I asked, my voice a raspy whisper.

Jake nodded. "A lot." He leaned back and took in a deep breath. "If I'm honest, I missed Magnolia. I missed Shari and Tag and Bella. I missed the small community feeling. The idea that everyone knew everyone." His voice drifted off as his gaze moved back to me. "But I missed you the most."

I couldn't help but stare at him. I felt as if I were dreaming. Never in a million years did I think that Jake would come back and say these things to me. I'd convinced myself that he'd moved on even if I couldn't.

And I wanted to be happy. I wanted to throw caution to the wind and love him like I'd wanted to do for so long —but I couldn't bring myself to do that. My mind feared what he would do to me if I let my heart take over. A part of me wanted to hold back.

What if I loved him like I wanted to? What if I trusted him again? Would he protect me? Or would he leave at the first sign of conflict?

Could I handle that kind of rejection again?

"Don't worry, Clem. I'm not expecting anything from you. I just…wanted to let you know where I stand. Where I will always stand. I'll be patient. I know it will take time." His voice lowered as he leaned in to catch my gaze. "I'm willing to put in the time."

I chewed my lip as I studied him. It was a relief that he didn't want me to make a decision right now. That he was going to give me the time I needed to figure out what I wanted to do.

But then fear washed over me as I realized that left everything in my court. I *was* going to have to make a decision about him—about us. And I wasn't sure I was ready for that.

It was one thing to live in the past. There was a certain safety in focusing on what had happened.

What scared me more than anything was that, now, the door was opened to the future. And the future I had no control over.

The future could hurt me.

More than I'd been hurt before.

13

SHARI

I felt lighter the entire day. The conversation that I had with Craig the night before mixed with the excitement for the party we were hosting at the inn, and I finally felt as if the nightmare that had been my life for the last few years was finally lifting.

It was as if my life were finally returning to normal.

And I didn't realize until I was gathering items for the party tonight that I missed normal. Bella and Tag seemed to notice the shift in my attitude. Bella was her normal chatty self, but Tag smiled at me. Twice.

It was as if this was what we'd needed to finally mend the broken family bonds that had been created when Craig and I were fighting. And the thought that we might be finally coming out of this long and dark tunnel put a smile on my face for the first time in days.

A genuine, happy smile. Something that I hadn't been

able to conjure up for a long time. But there it was. Plastered on my face and making me look like an idiot.

Maggie must have noticed because when I came into the inn at five with a big box in my arms and a smile on my face, she replied with a smile of her own. "Well, you look happy."

I chuckled as I followed her through the inn and out the back door. We descended the back steps and made our way over to the grill, which had a roaring fire inside of it. Archer was poking the coals with a stick while sweat beaded on his brow.

"I am happy," I said as I set the box of decorations down on one of the picnic tables.

"I bet. It must feel good to have your brother home." There was a reverence in Maggie's voice that got me intrigued.

"Do you not talk to your siblings?"

Maggie shook her head. "Only child. What I would have given to live with a brother or sister. If just to help deal with the craziness of parents." She chuckled.

I nodded. "Yeah, but you have to deal with them as punks when they were kids."

"Hey, I heard that," Jake said as he approached me and wrapped his arm around my shoulders before he gave me a noogie.

I swatted at his hands, but my brother had not only gotten bigger than me, but much stronger. I was helpless in this situation. Nothing I did could loosen his grasp on me. I poked and jabbed until I found his ribs, and he snapped back. Now that I was free, I went for any part of him that I could grab.

Jake just laughed and held me at bay like I was nothing more than a bug.

"Ahhh!" Bella's war cry sounded, and suddenly, she'd launched herself onto her uncle. He pretended to stagger and fall into the grassy section next to the grill, and it turned quickly into a wrestling match.

I laughed and straightened, raking my hands through my hair. I glanced around to find Tag watching Jake and Bella with a smile on his lips. It was small and faint, but it was there and it brought happiness to my soul. To see my baby opening up brought so much peace to my heart that I could cry.

"Everything okay?" Maggie asked.

I nodded as I began to pull out the streamers and bags of balloons that I'd bought. I set them on the table. Then I sat down and opened the bag and began to stretch out a balloon. "Yeah," I said. "You?"

She blew out her breath as she moved to sit across from me with her arms stretched out on the tabletop. "This whole running an inn business is a lot harder than I thought."

I studied her. She looked tired but happy. Something that I missed for myself. I had the tired part down, but it was the happiness that I was missing. Though I couldn't help but feel that maybe, just maybe, happiness was just around the corner for me.

"Are you excited for tonight?" she asked me, wiggling her eyebrows as her gaze swept over me.

My face heated as I nodded. "Yeah. Craig surprised me when he said he got us a room." I blew into the balloon I'd just finished stretching.

Maggie's smile turned soft as she studied me. "I'm happy for you."

I finished blowing up the balloon and tied the end and then started on the next one. Jake finished wrestling with Bella and moved to join me at the table. We chatted and blew up the balloons together until Clementine showed up.

Maggie went with her inside, and I watched as Jake's whole demeanor changed. He went from laughing and joking to quiet and tight-lipped when Clementine came around.

I peeked over at him while I finished blowing up the last balloon. He was staring a bit too hard at the streamers that he'd just pulled from their packaging.

"Everything okay?" I asked between blowing air into the balloon.

Jake startled and glanced over at me as if he hadn't expected me to speak. His eyes were wide, and he cleared his throat as he shifted. "Um, yeah."

I snorted, tied off the balloon, and then let it fall onto the pile we'd started. "Right." I stood and stretched, glancing down and wincing at the fact that the bench had left an imprint on my legs. "You forget that I was present when you and Clementine were a thing. I know when you are brooding over her." I raised my eyebrows as I grabbed the roll of tape and the first balloon and made my way over to the post of the gazebo and proceeded to affix the balloons to it.

Jake moved to help me, and I could tell that he was mulling over what I'd said. I finally grabbed a piece of tape and stuck it to his forearm. "Are you going to tell me, or do you need me to beat it out of you?"

Jake raised an eyebrow at me and moved to pull the tape from his arm. "Rude," he said as he bunched it up in his hand and tossed it onto the table. Then he sighed. "I guess we had a conversation earlier, and I'm not sure where Clementine landed on it."

I paused and turned to him, giving him my full attention. "A conversation?"

He nodded and continued taping up balloons like he'd didn't know that I was currently facing him. "A conversation."

I rolled my eyes at the cryptic manner in which my brother was speaking. "And? What was this conversation about?"

He sighed as his arms fell to his sides, and he turned to face me. "About us. About what I did. About how I'll wait and earn her trust." He looked at me and I could see the pain in his gaze. It was similar to the pain he'd felt when he left—except this time it was mixed with regret. The regret of realizing that what he'd done just might have ruined everything.

It was so powerful that I found my breath catching in

my throat. I studied him for a moment before I turned away and focused on decorating again. "And she didn't respond?"

"Not really." From the corner of my eye, I saw Jake moving to the next gazebo post and taping balloons to it. "She just kind of blew it off, and then we didn't talk about it for the rest of the time we were together."

"Why were you together?" I asked.

"We went across the bridge to buy food for tonight."

"And you had this soul-revealing discussion in a grocery store?"

Jake paused and then shook his head. "Naw. I took her to Jolly Time."

"You took her to an arcade?"

He nodded as he reached up to tape another balloon. "It was a place—"

"You went when you were dating, I know." I sighed as I grabbed the streamers and a nearby stool so that I could start stringing them. "So you were at this arcade and you just told her all of this? Was there any lead in?"

Jake was so quiet that I feared he'd left, and I was just talking to myself. But when I turned, I saw that he was staring at the balloon he was holding as if it was going to give him the answers he needed. It was strange. My brother was a confident guy. Valedictorian of his class and captain of the football team. This wasn't him. So unsure and confused. It almost made me feel sorry for him.

If he hadn't been the sole reason for his suffering.

"So what are you going to do?" I moved to lean against the stool so I could focus my attention on him.

Jake shrugged and moved to tape the last balloon up. "Wait for her to decide, I guess. I just don't know."

I nodded. "Well, you hurt her. You have to make sure that you do things on her timeline. It's what she deserves. If you love her, you'll let her heal on her own schedule." My heart squeezed at my words, and I realized how true those statements were. Suddenly, my happy evening with my husband changed.

Truth was, Craig had hurt me. Bad. And the fact that he thought he could just come back and pretend that nothing had happened hurt me. Everything seemed to be on his timetable, not mine. Even this evening at the hotel was all about him.

My stomach hurt as I turned away from Jake. I felt angry and betrayed—but mostly with myself. Since when had I turned into this critical wife? Craig was doing a good thing for me…right?

I shook my head and focused on putting up the streamers. After all, this was not the time or place to try to weed through my feelings for Craig. I was going to push those thoughts from my mind and focus on the party. I'd face whatever I felt about Craig and our situation later. Once we'd had time to talk about what had been taking place these last few months.

But until then, I was going to continue to believe that my marriage was saved and everything was going to turn around.

Suddenly, two arms surrounded me, and I was pulled down from the stool I was on. I yelped as Jake laughed and spun me in a circle. When he set me down, I turned around and whacked his arm. "What the crap." I demanded, feeling as if I just might vomit onto the ground. Once a woman reached a certain age, spinning just wasn't feasible for her anymore.

And I was there.

"Be happy," Jake said as he playfully punched my arm. "I didn't mean to bring you down with my issues. You seemed so happy when I walked up here, and now, you look as if I killed your dog."

His grin was contagious, and I couldn't help but smile back at him. "Fine," I said as I leaned into him and flicked his forehead. "I'll be happy."

He nodded and then turned and sprinted over to Tag, where he grabbed Tag's iPad and took off with it. Tag complained and charged after his uncle.

I sighed as I climbed back up onto the stool and finished hanging the streamers.

By six o'clock, everything was decorated and the meat was sizzling on the grill. Most of the partygoers were present and conversing while they waited for the food to finish. It was nice, having small talk with people that I knew and loved, but I was ready for Craig to show up. I was ready not to be single Shari.

Clementine spotted me, and a moment later, she came over to me and slung her arm around my shoulders. "Hey," she said, "having a good time?"

I nodded as I took one last sweep of the faces around me and then turned my attention back to her. "Just waiting for Craig to show up. Carol already picked up the kids."

"Craig is coming?"

I wasn't sure if I should be hurt at the tone of Clementine's voice. It was almost as if she were surprised that Craig would come. But I didn't want to make mountains out of molehills, even if my best friend's doubt only magnified my own.

"Yeah. He got a room for us tonight." I waved toward the inn.

Clementine raised her eyebrows. "He did?"

That felt like a dagger to my heart, but I brushed it off. Clementine didn't mean to hurt me. I had to keep telling myself that.

I nodded. "As a surprise and an apology for the way things have been the last few months." And then I decided to ask her a leading question. "Isn't that great?"

Clementine scoffed but then pressed her lips together and nodded. "It's great."

It was too late. Her attitude had already struck its intended target. There was no way I was going to stand around and allow her to cast doubt on my marriage. That wasn't what friends did. "I'm going to go refill my glass," I said as I pushed past her and over to the drink table despite her calls for me to come back. Just as I walked up, Victoria did as well.

Letting out my breath slowly, I nodded toward her. "Hey, Victoria."

She gave me a small, polite, and very Victoria smile. "Shari."

I waited for her to fill her glass and then step to the side for me to do the same. While I poured the punch into my cup, I peeked over at Victoria, who was still standing there. I furrowed my brow as I turned my attention back to my glass.

"Did you need something?" I asked as I turned to face her.

Victoria took a long drink before bringing her glass down and holding it in her hand. "I was wondering if I could come to your school sometime before summer break to talk to the kids."

I eyed her. "Why?"

She laughed, and it sounded as political and fake as always. "Well, it's an election year again, and I wanted to contact as many of my constituents as possible."

I stared at her. "You know there are only *kids* at my school."

She laughed again, this time the sound was more grating than before. "Of course, but if they see me and like me, then they'll talk to their parents."

She had to be joking, but before I could tell her that, I saw Craig walk up. Instead of standing there and talking to her more, I just nodded and threw, "Call the school to set it up. Just don't make it political," over my shoulder as I walked through the crowd to catch up with Craig.

"Hey, honey," I said as I walked up to him. I rose up onto my tiptoes to kiss him, but he pulled away to stare down at me. I couldn't help but feel hurt—after all, I wanted to prove to everyone here that things were fine, but he didn't seem to want to do the same.

Instead he just gave me a strained smile and then glanced around at the people by us. "When do you think you'll be done?" He sounded tired and drained, and it made me feel exhausted.

"I don't know. The food hasn't even come off the grill yet." It was hard, but I was able to downplay the bite in my tone. The happiness that I felt earlier in the day had waned, and reality was coming crashing down around me.

Craig sighed and pushed his hand through his hair. "I'm going to go get our room and take a nap, then." He glanced down and gave me a small smile before turning and heading to the inn.

I thought about calling after him, but I didn't have the energy. Instead, I downed the rest of my punch and headed to the bar to get something that might help dull the pain I was feeling inside.

And that's where I stayed until the last of the party-goers said goodnight to Jake and headed out. Archer and Maggie were walking around collecting garbage, and Clementine and Jake were packaging up the remaining food. I sighed as I pushed away from the bar and made my way toward them. I hadn't realized how much I'd drunk until I staggered a few times.

Sure, I felt buzzed, but I was determined to drink until

the pain of my marriage no longer afflicted me.

"Hey," Jake caught me on my third stagger.

The only thing that coursed through me was frustration for my situation and frustration for my brother. I moved to push him off me, but he just held me tighter. "Are you okay?" he asked.

I wiggled, but nothing I did released his grasp on me. "I'm fine," I said.

"Mags, can you get her some coffee?" I heard Clementine call to Maggie as Jake led me over to the picnic bench.

I twisted to tell Maggie that she didn't have to, but Jake had already pressed down on my shoulders, and the only option I had was to obey his directions and sit.

I sat under Clementine and Jake's scrutiny as I drank the cup of coffee that Maggie made me. When I was finished, I turned to face my friend and my brother and gave them a smile. "Happy?" I was annoyed that my buzz was already weakening. That forced me to feel the pain that I was so determined not to feel anymore.

They both raised their eyebrows at me and then looked at each other.

"Wanna tell me what this about?" I asked as I motioned to the three of us.

"What do you mean?" Jake asked. "We just wanted to make sure you were more sober before you walked right into the ocean and disappeared."

I snorted and tipped my head back. "Yeah right," I said as I glared at both of them again. "There's something else going on, and I doubt it's couples therapy."

Jake cursed under his breath as he glared at me. Good. I could feel that they wanted to say something to me. It was the same feeling I'd gotten ever since Jake walked through my door. It was judgement. It was pity. And all of it involved Craig and my marriage.

"We're just worried about you, Shari," Clementine said as she reached out and grabbed my hand.

That was the wrong move. "There's nothing to be worried about," I snapped back as I pulled my hand from her grasp.

"Hey," Jake said as he lifted his hand up, as if that was all it took to stop me.

"I don't have to listen to this," I said as I moved to stand. Jake's hands landed on my shoulders, and I was forced to sit again.

"We care about you, Shari. We want to help."

A volcano erupted inside of me. It was anger toward them and what they were doing right now. Anger toward the fact that I'd done a horrible job of faking happiness. And anger that they'd seen through it all and still felt like the best thing to do was confront me.

Couldn't they see that I was hurting here? Was the only thing that mattered to them placation of their guilty feelings because their friend and sister was a loser in a loser marriage?

Well, I didn't have time for this. If I was going to fix what was wrong in my life, then I needed to leave. Right now.

"I'm leaving," I said, and when Jake moved to push me

down again, I swatted his hands away. "Stop." I glared at him, and thankfully that was all it took for him to back down.

I stood and stomped across the lawn and up to the back door of the inn. Once inside, I collapsed against the nearby wall. I wanted to say it was because I was still tipsy, but that conversation had sobered me up.

Tears sprang to my eyes, and I did everything I could to muscle them down. What had started out as a good day had gone sour so fast that I had whiplash. I dipped my head down and allowed a sob to escape.

Everyone was turning on me. Tag. Craig. And now Clementine and Jake. Pretty soon, Bella would turn as well, and I would be left all alone.

And I was pretty sure that when that happened, it would all be over for me.

There was no coming back from losing everyone you loved.

I wiped at my cheeks and stood, clearing my throat. Feeling self-pity wasn't going to fix anything. If I wanted things to change, it needed to start with me.

So what if I lost Jake and Clementine? If I could make my marriage work, then at least I had my family. And that was what we were here to do tonight.

Make our marriage work.

That was what I was going to do. Come hell or high water, I would make my marriage work.

CLEMENTINE

I swallowed back the sobs as I finished gathering up the party items and shoved them into the trunk of my car. I didn't care if things spilled or rolled around when I drove. I just needed to get out of here as fast as I could.

No matter what I did, I could still see Shari's disappointment and betrayal when she'd looked at us. I could still see the hurt written all over her face, and it was like a punch to my gut every time I closed my eyes.

In my effort to help my friend, I'd hurt her.

Jake attempted to talk to me, but one look from me and he kept his distance.

As soon as I got home, I collapsed on my couch and buried my face in the cushion. I screamed into the fabric in an effort to release all of my pent-up anger and anxiety.

It didn't help.

Frustrated, I flipped to my back and stared up at the

ceiling above me. Tears filled my eyes as I realized that I may have ruined one of my oldest friendships. Shari was hurt and betrayed by what we'd done. I could see it written on her face and hear it in the inflection of her voice.

And not only did I basically tell her that her marriage was crap, but that she didn't have the support of the two people in her life that should have her back.

It was like I'd hit six feet down and kept digging.

I draped my arm over my face and allowed the tears to fall. Shari had been there for me when I'd had to put Dad in the home. She invited me over when I felt lonely. I was supposed to support her, and yet, I did the exact opposite.

The sound of three knocks on the door caused me to lower my arm. Was it Shari? And then I felt dumb. Of course it wasn't Shari. What did I think? That she would follow me back here to tell me that she understand why I did what I did and that she forgave me?

Gah, I was an idiot.

But who else knew where we kept the spare key to access the building?

The knocks sounded again. I slowly rolled off the couch and padded over to the door. "What?" I said as I yanked the door open while the visitor was in the middle of another knock.

I glared up at Jake, who was staring down at me with wide eyes. I folded my arms across my chest and stared at him. He held up a six-pack of beers and nodded toward them.

I grabbed them, and before he could come in, I slammed the door in his face. If he hadn't convinced me to confront Shari, none of this would have happened.

I leaned against the door and tipped my head back, closing my eyes. Truth was, I didn't want to be alone tonight, but I also didn't want to be around Jake either. It was this strange push and pull that left me feeling raw and exposed.

"Clem." Jake's voice carried through the door.

My heart instantly picked up speed. I shook my head as the desire to open the door and let him in grew stronger. I wasn't going to give in this easily. I had at least a little self-respect.

"Please, talk to me," he said.

The desperation in his voice caused the desire to take it away to rise up inside of me. All I could think about was wrapping my arms around him and comforting him despite the fact that, right now, he was the only person I could hate.

"I'll stay out here all night if I have to," he murmured. I heard a thud, and the door shifted as if he'd just pressed all his weight against it like I was.

I turned and spread my hand out on the door, wondering if I waited long enough, could I feel his warmth? I closed my eyes and imagined what he looked like in the small and cramped hallway, leaning against the door, waiting for me. It caused all the emotions that I'd been so desperate to keep at bay to rise up inside of me.

But I couldn't just let him in. Not into my house, and

not into my heart. I feared that as soon as I did, there would be no getting him out again.

"I left once, I won't do it again," he said so softly that I had to press my ear against the door to catch every word.

"Jake," I whispered. His meaning wasn't lost on me. My heart surged and I didn't stop myself this time. Instead, I pushed off the door and turned the handle.

Jake must not have anticipated that I might actually open the door. As soon as I took away his support, he fell right into my apartment. It was like watching something in slow motion.

I tried to reach out to catch him, but that was a joke. Instead, I went down with him and landed on top of him while he sprawled onto the ground with a resounding thud.

"Ouch," he moaned as he lay there.

"I'm so sorry," I said as I scrambled to get off him. He wrapped his hands around my upper arms and held me there as if he didn't want me to go anywhere. I hesitated and then peered up at him to see what was going on.

"Just lie here with me," he said. His eyes were closed, and his expression was one that I couldn't read.

He didn't look like he was in pain or suffering from a concussion. Instead, he was stoic as he lay there. Realizing that there was no way I was going to break the hold he had on me, I moved my right hand to the floor and used it to help prop my body up.

Jake didn't move his hands from either arm. Instead, the warmth of his skin against mine felt as if it were pulsating through my body with each beat of my heart. Then, suddenly, he tipped his body and I slipped to the floor. He kept his hold on me until my head was lying on his arm. Then he used his other arm to cage me in as he turned to his side and pulled me to his chest.

I stared his cotton shirt as we lay there. The material looked so soft that, before I could stop myself, I extended my fingers and let them graze the fabric. That caused a low rumble to erupt in his throat and rattle his chest.

"Don't do that," he said in a gruff tone that caused goosebumps to rise up on my skin. As if to emphasize his desire to get me to stop, he reached down and cocooned my hand with his.

I felt frozen in place as he continued to hold me as if it were as easy as breathing, though for me it was anything but. My breath was haggard. My heart felt as if it were going to beat from my chest. I was pretty sure he could feel the effect he was having on me, and yet it didn't seem as if it bothered him.

My mind was swimming, and my body was going haywire. This was anything but relaxing. How could he be so calm?

"Jake?" I finally managed out.

Jake tightened his grip on my hand for a moment before he released it. "Hmm?" he asked, as if that was as good of an answer as *yes*.

"Why did you come here?" I pushed up with my free hand so that I was leaning over him. My hair fell down one side of my face and brushed the ground next to his head. That must have been the magic move that woke him up because, a second later, his eyes were open and he was staring at me.

It wasn't until I felt the intensity of his stare that I realized I was inches away from his face. Inches away from his lips. And like a moth to the flame, I glanced down at his glorious mouth. All the memories of what it felt like to kiss him surrounded me.

My body yearned to be touched like it once had been. The familiarity of his calloused hands across my skin was a memory that I may have replayed a few times since he left. He knew me and I knew him. I was sure that kissing him wouldn't feel the same. It would feel deeper, more meaningful.

"I was worried about you," he said. His voice had deepened, and it sent shivers down my spine.

I watched as his gaze dip to my lips and then back up to my eyes. Then, slowly, he reached out and tucked my hair behind my ear.

"I didn't want to leave you like that. Not when I saw you hurting." His fingers lingered in my hair, his hand cupping my cheek. "I ran once, I didn't want to do it again."

Suddenly, his thumb brushed my lips. It was soft and warm as he traced the sensitive skin. My body numbed and ached simultaneously at the touch. My eyes darted down to his lips as the control that I had on my desires waned.

"Jake," I whispered as he moved his hand to the back of

my head and slowly lifted his head to mine.

"Clementine," he growled as I met him the rest of the way, our lips crashing into each other like waves on the beach during a summer rain.

All the walls that I'd built up to protect me from this man came crumbling down as I lost myself in the feeling of his lips against mine and the warmth of his arms wrapped around me. He pulled himself to sitting, which brought us closer together, deepening the kiss.

His tongue teased my lips open. We fell into a dance where each moment, each breath, deepened the kiss we were experiencing.

My hands found their way from his chest, up to his shoulders, and then entangled themselves into his hair. He growled and pulled me closer, and I responded by slipping onto his lap. My arms tightened around him as if my soul feared that if I let him go, he would leave forever.

"We need to stop," Jake said as he pulled away and gently lowered me to the ground.

I whimpered as I watched him back away from me. He leaned against the wall with his knees up and an arm resting on top of them.

"I'm sorry," I said through the hazy fog of kissing him. My lips felt swollen and puffy as I chewed on them.

Jake studied me for a moment before he scoffed and looked to the side. "You need to stop doing that," he said, his voice deep with intention.

"Doing what?"

He glanced back at me with a fire in his gaze that I'd

never seen before. As if there was nothing that was going to keep him from me but sheer will.

"Biting your lip. Touching my shirt." He sighed as he leaned his head back and closed his eyes. "Existing."

I chuckled as I reached over and pulled a beer from the six pack that he'd brought. "Existing?"

He nodded. "Your existence drives me crazy."

I popped the top of the beer and then grabbed another one and scooted over until I was sitting next to him. I purposely brushed his arm with mine as I handed over the extra can. "I brought you one."

He growled again as he shifted over until we were no longer touching. "I mean it, Clem." He took the beer from me, popped the tab, and drank half of it before I could think of a comeback.

"Does this bother you?" I asked as I reached out and ran my fingers up and down his forearm.

His gaze dropped to my fingers, and I felt every muscle in his arm tighten. Goosebumps rose up on his skin, and I giggled as I reveled in the fact that I could make him react like this. It was a superpower that I was most definitely going to exploit.

"Clementine," he said in a deep and gravelly voice. Suddenly, he reached out and engulfed my hand with his, effectively stilling me. He then stared at his hand for a moment before he slipped it around and entwined my fingers with his. Then he brought my hand up and pressed his lips to it.

I laughed as I snuggled in closer to him and rested my

head on his shoulder. He was stiff at first but then began to slowly relax. He stretched out his arm, taking mine with it, until our entwined hands were resting on his thigh. I closed my eyes for a moment as I reveled in the feeling of my body next to Jake's.

It felt so right. It felt so familiar. It felt like home.

"I've dreamed about this moment for so long," he said as he tipped his head toward me and pressed his lips to my hair.

I could feel his warm breath on my skin, and it sent tingles throughout my body. "You have?" I asked as I squeezed his hand with my own.

He nodded and I felt every movement.

"You don't have very exciting dreams," I said as I tipped my face up to study him.

He furrowed his brow and then smiled at me. "I would have to agree."

I raised my head up and parted my lips. I broke our clasped hands and punched his shoulder as I began to pull away. "Hey," I said as I attempted to stand.

But Jake grabbed hold of my hand and pulled me back down onto him. I squirmed, but he held me tight as he brought me close to his chest. His lips found mine, and suddenly, I forgot everything that we had been talking about as I pulled him closer to me, deepening the kiss.

When I felt as if I were falling and I was never going to stop, Jake pulled back, his breathing matching the same cadence as my own. He rested his forehead against mine as he chuckled.

"You never let me finish," he said.

I parted my lips to speak, but he just met my words with another kiss. When he pulled back, he gave me a serious look.

"What I wanted to say was, the real thing is so much better." He reached up to tuck my hair behind my ear. "You, here, in my arms is so much better than any dream."

I wrinkled my nose at his cheesiness, but I didn't pull away. Instead, I leaned my head against his shoulder once more and entwined my fingers with his.

We sat there for hours, filling the time with conversation mixed with kisses. It was as if we'd never been apart, and yet, everything felt new. We were different people now, both trying to navigate what our renewed relationship meant.

At some point in the night, I fell asleep, and it wasn't until I felt Jake lower me down onto my bed that I woke up. Not wanting him to leave and not wanting to be alone, I grabbed ahold of his arm.

"Stay," I whispered as I stared up at him. His eyes widened and I shook my head. "Not like that. Just stay with me tonight." I patted the bed. "Just hold me."

I turned to my side to show him that there was room for him to lie down. I closed my eyes and wondered if he would actually take me up on it or if I was crazy to think that he would want to spend more time with me.

But then the bed shifted a few seconds later, and his arms were wrapped around me, drawing me against his chest. My entire body melted into the warmth that he emanated. This was exactly where I belonged. Being wrapped inside of Jake's embrace was what I'd been looking for all this time and hadn't found until this moment.

In this moment, the only person that mattered was Jake. The only thing that mattered was how I felt about him.

And in this moment, I was truly happy. For the first time in a very long time, I felt like this was where I belonged.

I was home.

SHARI

I stumbled into the room, anger still clinging to me like a cold I couldn't shake. I'd hoped that my walk inside would help cool me down, but it hadn't. I was just as angry as I'd been when I stormed away from the two people I'd once called my friends and now called my enemies.

They'd broken my heart and abandoned me. So from now on, they were dead to me.

Craig seemed uninterested in me when I found him lying on the king-sized bed. Instead of even acknowledging me, he kept his gaze focused on his phone, watching what I could only assume was some ridiculous cartoon show that I would never understand the appeal of.

That only fueled the anger raging inside of me. How could he turn to a phone when I was standing right in front of him? I glowered at him, angry that his behavior had led my friends to host that ridiculous intervention.

Not wanting to be around Craig right now and needing a moment to cool down, I declared that I was going to shower and that I expected whatever he was watching would be over by the time I got out.

Craig just gave me a quick grunt and flipped to his side. I sighed as I glared in his direction and then headed into the bathroom, where I locked the door. I didn't want any surprises that included him jumping into the shower with me. With the way I was feeling, I was more likely to remove certain appendages if they came my direction than embrace them.

As the hot water sprayed around me, hitting my muscles and filling the room with steam, I began to realize that Craig and I had a lot of things to talk about if we were going to even attempt to make this work. What had been happening over the last few months wasn't going to be solved by a stay at Magnolia Inn.

The hurt and betrayal went a lot deeper than a mere conversation could fix.

I wrapped a towel around my hair and body and stepped out of the shower. I took my time applying my face lotion and dressing in my silk pajamas before I came out. When I pulled open the door, I found Craig lying on the bed with his phone resting on his chest and his mouth open, snoring.

I scoffed and rolled my eyes as I continued to towel dry my hair. I wandered over to the small table and chair in the corner and plopped down. I brought my feet up to rest on the seat of the chair and tipped my head back and closed my eyes.

If I could just block out the sound of Craig and pretend that I was here alone, this might be the vacation that I so desperately needed. And then realization washed over me. I wanted to be here…without Craig.

What kind of wife says that about her husband? What kind of wife wants to live a life separate from her husband because being with him is too much work?

Tears began to form in my eyes as I straightened my head and used the towel to dab at my eyes. "Me," I whispered. I was that wife. Something was so broken in our marriage that I no longer wanted to spend the kind of time with him that a wife should.

My gaze found its way over to Craig, and I studied him for a moment. Thoughts of Bella and Tag entered my mind. I knew the reason why I stuck around. They were small and young and would be devastated if I walked away from their father.

It would require them to decide who to live with and who to side with. And as much as I didn't want them to have to do that, it was a natural consequence of divorce. And I wasn't sure that I could ask that of them.

I stood and walked over to my overnight bag and pulled out my wide-toothed comb. I was in the midst of brushing my hair when I heard Craig's phone chime. I paused, glancing over my shoulder in its direction.

Craig didn't move. Instead he grunted and turned,

allowing the phone to slide off his chest and onto the bed. My gaze was focused on it, and I startled when it chimed again.

Curiosity won over, and I tiptoed to the bed. After all, it was ten at night. Who was messaging him?

I quietly reached across the bed and grabbed his phone. He shifted the moment I touched it, and I paused with my heart pounding, waiting for him to catch me and pull the phone away—but he didn't. Instead, he released a loud snore and continued sleeping.

I hurriedly pulled the phone from the bed, crossed the room, and locked myself into the bathroom. Now alone, I glanced down at the screen just to have my entire body turn ice cold.

It was a text. From some person—and really, I could only assume it was a girl—with a message for my husband.

Missy: I miss you. How long are you—

I stared at the words. The three little words that I never thought I would discover on my husband's phone from another woman. Three little words that only confirmed what I'd feared. What I'd attempted to pretend didn't exist. I'd wanted to believe our marriage wasn't struggling because Craig was cheating on me, but because we were drifting apart.

But now, I realized that the reason we were so distant was because there was a gigantic wedge called *cheating* shoved between us.

I scoffed and tossed his phone onto the counter. I

pressed both hands down next to the sink and tipped my head forward. What had once been feelings of sadness and tears of worry, were now blinding rage. I couldn't believe this man would do this to me. To our family.

I cursed under my breath as I picked up the soap and chucked it into the shower. It bounced off the wall and ricocheted back into the room. I had to jump to the side for it to narrowly miss me.

Realizing that the person I should be hurting was not myself or the bathroom, but the snoring slug on the bed, I grabbed his phone, unlocked the door, and marched into the room.

I threw his phone onto the bed and then grabbed the blanket he was sleeping on. After a few tugs and a shove from my foot, he flipped onto the floor. I waited as he let out a groan and then rose up onto all fours, cursing while he moved.

"What the hell, Shari?" he asked when he finally straightened and turned to glare at me.

My entire body felt like a volcano that was moments away from exploding. And this time, I wasn't going to suppress it. He was going to know exactly what I thought of him and exactly where I thought he could shove his vows, his love, and our marriage.

"Who's Missy?" I asked through the controlled breathing I was attempting. I wanted him to know that I knew. That his lie was no longer secret.

He paused, his eyebrows rising and his lips pinched shut. His gaze swept the room and landed on his phone. I nodded and motioned toward it. "Go ahead, pick it up. We'll read what that tramp has to say together." I glowered at him and watched as he lunged across the bed and grabbed hold of it.

Then he straightened and cleared his throat as he adjusted his shirt. "She's a banker in Newport."

I scoffed and threw my hands into the air. I dropped my gaze because staring at him only infuriated me more. "How long?"

When he didn't respond right away, my anger only grew. I glared up at him as I pushed my hands through my hair. "How long, Craig?"

He shifted his weight and sighed. "Since January."

I screamed. Out loud and shrill. It was the first time I'd done that in a very long time. I'd spent most of my life being the calm one. Being the person that was cool and collected for everyone else around me. After all, that was my job. People depended on me.

But right now, I didn't want to be calm and collected. I was angry and hurt and felt as if a part of me was breaking. I was watching my family crumble in front of me, and there was nothing I could do to stop it.

Craig looked startled by my scream. He hunched over as he watched me with wide eyes as if he were trying to understand what I was going to do. Rage filled my chest, and I lunged at him with my fists flying.

I struck his chest a few times before his hands surrounded my upper arms and held me out at arm's length. He kept trying to dip his head down to meet my gaze, but I wasn't interested in any of that. Instead, I continued to fight for him to let me go.

I was hurting, and I was determined to make Craig hurt like I did.

"You have to stop this," Craig yelled.

Tears were flowing down my face as I pulled back, snapping his grip on me. I pushed my hair from my face and stared him down. Silence filled the room, similar to the calm that happens in the eye of the storm. The world was raging around us, but in this moment, there was quiet.

Until Craig's phone chimed. The same ringtone that sounded earlier. Both of us turned to his phone, which had been flung to the floor. I jumped at it, but Craig beat me. He hurriedly tucked the phone into his back pocket, and it was in that moment that I realized that I was finished with him.

I was over this. Craig. Me. Our marriage. I was done. In fact, I'd been done for a long time—I'd just been too scared to face it. I threw my hair back into a ponytail, grabbed my overnight bag, and slung it over my shoulder.

"I'm done," I said as I moved past him and over to the door.

"Shari?" Craig asked as he reached out and grabbed my upper arm.

I whipped it away, breaking his hold on me. "Let me go," I growled as I glanced up to glare at him.

He stepped back as he studied me. "What are you going to do?"

"It's not what I'm going to do, it's what you are going to do." I stepped toward him, and he responded by stepping back. "You are moving out. You are leaving Magnolia. You are going to leave me and the kids alone." I glared at him. "I'll be sending you divorce papers, so find another place to live." I jutted my finger in his direction.

Then I glared one last time at my loser of a husband and turned and stormed out of the room. Once I was safely out in the hall and the door to the room was shut, I collapsed against the wall and took in a few deep breaths.

Even though I knew I'd done the right thing, it still felt as if a million bricks were crushing my body. It felt as if I could barely breathe, and every muscle shook like an aftershock of an earthquake.

It took a few minutes and a lot of deep breaths for me to finally feel strong enough to stand. When I got down to Maggie's room, I knocked on the door. She emerged with a glass of wine in hand and wearing a robe. I could see Archer in the background, resting on the armchair in the corner.

"Sorry to bother you," I said through sobs. I attempted to wipe the tears away, but I feared that I just smeared everything around on my face.

Maggie shook her head, set her glass down, and wrapped me up into a hug. "It's okay," she said as she patted my back. "Archer, fix up a room for Shari." Maggie pulled back and patted me on the shoulders. "We'll take care of you. You just relax," she said as she led me over to the chair that Archer had been sitting on and pushed me to sit.

I complied.

I wasn't sure how long I sat there for, but eventually, Archer and Maggie came back and helped me into a room on the third floor. I rinsed my face and was climbing into bed right when Maggie knocked on the door again. She delivered some cookies and hot chocolate and told me to relax.

I pulled the covers up to my chin after consuming all of the cookies at a very unladylike rate, and buried myself in the pillows and comforter. I let the tears flow until I was sure there wasn't any more water left in my body.

Exhausted and ready to get this day over with, I closed my eyes and allowed darkness to take over.

For tonight, I was going to allow myself to feel pity for my situation. For tonight, I was going to grieve the marriage that I'd lost. For tonight, I was going to be weak.

Come tomorrow, all of this self-pity needed to end. Tomorrow, I needed to be strong for my children and for myself.

No matter how much I cried—no matter how much I ached—my life was changing. And there was nothing I could do about that.

My marriage was over.

For good.

CLEMENTINE

The early morning sun streamed into the room, waking me up. I squinted as I glanced at the window and then shifted so I could grab my phone and peer down at it.

Nine in the morning.

I sighed, and just as I did, someone shifted next to me in the bed.

I startled and glanced over to see Jake was there. I almost screamed as I took in his tousled hair and stilled features. Not wanting him to wake up to my bed head and drool-crusted face, I stealthily slipped out from under the covers and tiptoed out of the room.

Once I got into the bathroom, I shut the door and stared at myself in the mirror.

Memories of the night before came back to me, and I couldn't help but smile at my reflection. The feeling of Jake's lips on my own. The feeling of completeness that I felt being wrapped in his arms. All of those moments came rushing back to me and made me feel lightheaded and happy.

It was something I hadn't felt in a long time.

I quickly washed my face and patted my skin dry. Then I applied some mascara and lip gloss. Once I didn't look like a walking zombie anymore, I found my phone and texted Michelle to make sure that she was going to open the store.

When she sent back a thumbs-up, I hurried from the bathroom and into the kitchen, where I got started on making breakfast and coffee.

By the time the smell of bacon and eggs mixed with the aroma of freshly brewed coffee, Jake emerged from my room. He squinted around, and when his gaze landed on me, his smile widened.

"I'll wash up and be right back out," he said as he slipped into the bathroom and shut the door.

I nodded as I filled our plates and then brought them over to the table. I'd just poured two mugs of coffee when the bathroom door opened and Jake came out. He didn't hesitate to wrap his arms around me, pinning me between his body and the counter.

He nuzzled my neck through my hair, and shivers rushed down my skin when he inhaled. "Good morning," he said, his voice deep and gruff.

I nodded, my heart going haywire from his proximity. "Did you sleep well?" I asked as I twisted around so that I was facing him.

He pressed his lips to my neck and kissed a trail up to my ear to nibble on my earlobe. Then he pulled back and nodded. "Best sleep I've gotten in a long time." He furrowed his brow. "You?"

My lips tipped up into the smile that I could no longer fight. I entangled my fingers in his hair and pulled myself closer to him. He responded by dipping down until his lips were centimeters from mine.

"Yes." I nodded and then pressed my lips to his.

Jake wrapped his arms around my waist and lifted me up to sit on top of the counter. I wrapped my legs around him and pulled him next to me. I wasn't sure how long we kissed for, but when he finally let go of me and stepped back, I felt incomplete and cold. I glowered at him, to which he just laughed and helped me down.

"As much fun as that is, we do need to eat."

I sighed and nodded as we each grabbed our mugs of coffee and made our way over to the table. It didn't take us long to devour the food on our plates, and once they were empty, we both sat back, sipping on our coffee.

My thoughts returned to Shari and our conversation with her last night. My stomach instantly twisted into knots, and I scrunched my nose in an effort to stop the pain. I'd disappointed and hurt my best friend, and I wasn't sure if she would ever forgive me.

"Shari will come around," Jake said, breaking my thoughts.

I glanced up at him and parted my lips. "How did you…?"

He chuckled. "You forget I know more about you than *you* know about you," he said as he took another drink of his coffee.

I glowered at him, frustrated that he could still read me like a book. But then I sighed. Truth was, he'd hit the nail on the head. I wanted to believe what he said—that she would forgive me—but there was a part of me that said that wasn't going to be the case. That I'd royally ruined things for her and me.

After all, I'd basically been prepared to tell her that her husband was a prick and she should leave him. I buried my face into the crook of my arm and shook my head. *I would hate me if I were her.*

"I don't think she will," I mumbled into my arm.

Jake's chair scraped against the floor, and suddenly, his arms wrapped around me, pulling me to him. "We'll find a way. If there's anything I know about Shari, it's that she has a hard time holding a grudge." He leaned back and stared down at me. "We just need to give her time to work through it."

I nodded as I played with the soft folds of his shirt. "You're right. It's just hard."

I hated it when people didn't like me. I took it as my personal responsibility to make sure everyone got along and everyone was happy. The fact that I couldn't rush to fix things with Shari bothered me, but I knew it was what I needed to do.

If I cared enough about Shari, I would allow her to

come to me when she was ready and not force her when she wasn't.

It wasn't going to be easy, but I was going to do it. For my best friend.

Shari

It felt strange to wake up the next morning in my own room at the inn. The sun was streaming through the window, and the smell of fresh sheets and salt water wafted around me. Even though my entire body ached along with my soul, if I was going to sever ties with my spouse, this was the place I wanted to do it.

I snuggled deeper into the covers, pulling the blanket up to my neck and closing my eyes. Maybe if I lay here long enough, I would fall back asleep.

I hadn't realized how exhausted I was until I slept as hard as I had. The stress of the unknown was finally shaken by the truth. Even though I wasn't sure how things were going to play out or what my future looked like, I knew that the lies were going to stop. Craig's infidelity was out in the open, and I could lean on that truth for a while.

The days of living in the dark were over even if the thought of living in the light terrified me beyond belief.

Realizing that there was no way I was going to be able to sleep with my mind racing at a hundred miles an hour,

I pulled off the covers and sat up. I grabbed my phone and texted Carol, letting her know that I'd be home around noon.

She responded that she was going to take the kids to the ocean and for me and Craig to enjoy ourselves and not hurry back. I thanked her and set the phone on the nightstand.

I contemplated telling her that Craig and I were finished but then decided against it. I knew I was going to have to have that conversation with a lot of people, and I wasn't quite ready to start that today.

Today was about relaxation before reality.

After a long bubble bath, I dried off and dressed in a t-shirt and jeans. Something comfortable and freeing. I pulled my hair up into a bun and opened the door. I startled when I glanced up to see Maggie standing there with her hand raised as if she were about to knock.

Feeling like an idiot for giving her a front-row seat to my breakdown yesterday, I offered her a sympathetic smile. "Sorry," I said as I stepped out into the hall and shut the door behind me.

Maggie furrowed her brow as she shook her head. "There's nothing to be sorry about." She smiled as she extended her hand toward the stairs. "I was on my way to see if you want to join me for breakfast. Archer found a chef we are trying out, and I'd love a second opinion."

I glanced in the direction she motioned and then nodded as my stomach growled. "That sounds amazing," I said as I followed after her.

On our way down the stairs, Maggie turned to smile at me. "Did you sleep well?"

I nodded. "Amazing. Better than I have in months."

She grinned. "I'm glad to hear that." We kept the same pace as we descended. Just before we reached the bottom, she paused and faced me. "Craig checked out this morning," she said quietly as she leaned in.

My stomach sank. I wasn't ready to talk about him, and yet it seemed as if he were going to follow me despite my desire. "Really?"

Maggie nodded and then locked her lips. "I just wanted to let you know that you have the freedom to roam without fear of running into him. This is the only time I'll bring him up." She smiled softly, and I couldn't help but feel at ease in her presence.

"Thanks," I said as I followed her into the kitchen, where all sorts of mouth-watering smells were coming from.

There was a small breakfast nook in the corner, and Maggie motioned toward it. "We can sit. Brett will be here any moment with some food."

I obeyed and pulled out a chair to settle into.

"We're ready," Maggie called to the man whose back was to us.

"Yep," he called out, his voice deep. Then he turned and gave both of us a wide, perfectly formed smile.

I glanced over at Maggie, who was smiling at me. Brett brought two plates over to us with two perfectly cooked eggs benedict. The sauce that was drizzled over the eggs and English muffins smelled delectable.

Maggie and I began to eat. The food was so delicious that I finished everything he brought us. We ate in silence until we both leaned back, stretching out our stomachs and patting our tummies.

"That was incredible," Maggie said as Brett set down some freshly squeezed orange juice.

I nodded my appreciation. Brett just chuckled. "Just trying to prove that I'm perfect for the job."

Maggie dragged her fork through some of the leftover syrup on her plate. "Well, I can't speak for Archer, but it's a 10 out of 10 for me." Then Maggie glanced in my direction.

I smiled. "Same for me, although I'm not sure my opinion matters in this instance."

Brett thanked us and then started cleaning up. Maggie grabbed her orange juice and stood. "Let's move out onto the porch," she said.

Not wanting to be alone right now, I followed after her.

Once outside, the warm, salty air surrounded me, and I closed my eyes for a moment as the breeze rushed over me. Then, feeling like an idiot, I opened my eyes and moved to sit across from Maggie. She was leaning her head against the back of her chair and rocking ever so slightly as she stared out at the ocean.

I settled down next to her and found myself staring out in the same direction. There was something so relaxing about sitting here with nothing to do and no one but myself to worry about.

We sat in silence for a few minutes before Maggie sighed and glanced over at me. She offered me a small smile. "What do you think about the inn? Do you think that I've got something good here? Or am I insane?" She took a sip of her orange juice and focused back on the ocean.

I nodded. "It's great. I have no doubt that as soon as the word gets out about this place, it will be swamped."

She glanced down at the glass in her hands. "This is so crazy. Just a year ago it felt like everything in my life was failing." She paused, shaking her head as if she were trying to dispel her thoughts, and then took a drink of juice.

"What were you doing last year?" It sounded nice to just sit back and listen to someone else's story for a while. It would help distract me from the crapshoot that was my life.

"I was getting a divorce." She said the words so matter-of-factly that I was taken aback at first. How could she say that in that way? As if it didn't matter anymore.

Curiosity got the better of me, and I found myself leaning in to hear more. "What happened?" Maggie glanced over at me, and I raised my hand. "You don't have to tell me if you don't want to."

Maggie smiled and shook her head. "No, it's okay. I don't mind talking about it." She sighed. "Even though it felt like such a big hurdle for me to overcome at the time, when I look back at it, I have a hard time remembering any of it." She furrowed her brow. "It's like, I know it hurt me and that I should feel hurt, but I don't."

"Like childbirth," I responded with a snort.

Maggie chuckled. "I wouldn't know, although I hope to find out someday." She got a far-off look in her eyes and her cheeks hinted pink.

I nodded as I remembered the pain that Archer went through not only with the loss of his daughter, but the destruction of his marriage. "I hope so too. Archer deserves a do-over."

Maggie pinched her lips together as her gaze drifted down to her lap. Then she smiled back up at me. "And you do too."

I studied her, tears welling up in my eyes at her words. They meant a lot, especially coming from someone who'd been through what I was about to go through and had made it out intact. It was something that I wanted to aspire to.

"You think so?" I asked as I angrily swiped at the tears that decided to roll down my cheeks. I was annoyed that at the mention of being able to move on, my body responded this way.

Maggie reached out and patted my hand. "I know so." She smiled. "If I can survive, anyone can survive. At least here, you have the support of your kids, Clementine, and Jake. That's more than I had."

I studied her. I wished I hadn't exploded on my brother and friend yesterday. But I had, and I knew before

I could lean on them for anything, I was going to have to admit I was wrong.

"I kind of exploded on them yesterday," I said, embarrassed to admit to my bad behavior out loud.

Maggie chuckled. "I know that feeling all too well. I lost a lot of friends during my divorce. But what I was left with were those who were truly there for me no matter what." She leaned over. "I have a feeling that Clementine and Jake are the lifelong kind of friends."

"I would hope Jake is. He's kind of stuck with me forever."

"I think Clementine feels the same," Maggie said as she leaned back and closed her eyes. Her lips were tipped up into a satisfied smile. "I think we both will have a hard time ever succeeding at getting rid of Clementine no matter what we do."

I laughed. "She does have a tendency to stick to you."

Maggie nodded. "But it's a good thing. There needs to be people like that in the world for people like us."

I sighed as I settled back into my chair. My orange juice was warming, so I drank the rest of it and then set the glass down next to me. I rocked a few times, closing my eyes to focus on the motion and the sound of the waves as they broke against the shore.

I couldn't help but feel at peace as I sat there, relaxing. Talking to Maggie had helped me immensely. Not only with how I felt about my present situation, but with the hope I felt for the future.

Things were looking up for the first time in a very

long time, and even though I was certain that I was in for a rocky ride, I knew I had a lot of people in my corner willing to back me up when I needed it.

I just needed to apologize for what I'd said, and I would officially be on my way to changing out my current situation for a much better one.

Sitting here, looking at how healed Maggie was, gave me the confidence to know that someday, I was going to be just happy as she was.

And I couldn't wait.

CLEMENTINE

Monday morning rolled around and Shari still hadn't called. I paced in my room all of Sunday night with my phone in my hand and her number on the screen. All I needed to do was press the green talk button, and I would have called her—I just couldn't find the strength.

I knew how angry she was with me. I'd hurt her. I'd gone behind her back and ganged up on her with her brother, of all people. If I were her, I'd hate me too.

I sighed as I hugged my knees. I was sitting at the register with my feet propped up on the shelf in front of me, and I was leaning forward and staring out the window. It was exceptionally slow today. Which only made things worse. It gave me more time to think about what I'd done wrong and made me feel even guiltier.

My phone chimed next to me. I glanced over to see that it was an email from Magnolia Bank. My heart quickened pace as I lifted up my phone and swiped at the screen to bring it up.

Congratulations, Ms. Ramsey,

You have been approved for a $400,000 loan.

Please contact Kevin Malone for further information.

My heart was pounding as I read over the words. I couldn't help but stare at the loan amount and the word *congratulations*. It was like, for the first time, all of my dreams were coming true.

Like I was finally seeing the sun break through the rain clouds that were my life. This was the first time I was approved to do anything, much less fulfill a dream I'd had since I was a teen.

I couldn't help but feel as if my life were just starting.

I closed the email and pressed the contact button on my phone. Shari's number was pulled up before I could stop myself. Just as I moved to press the talk button, I stopped.

Right.

Shari was mad at me. And no matter how much I wished that wasn't true, it didn't make a difference. She'd stormed out on me and walked away. If I cared about her like I did, I would wait until she was ready to talk to me before I confronted her.

So I scrolled back to Maggie's name and selected it. Three rings in, she answered.

"Hey, Clem," she said. She sounded out of breath.

"Everything okay?" I asked.

She chuckled. "Just cleaning."

I nodded as I leaned back, hooking my arm around my legs to keep myself balanced on the barstool. "I got good news," I sang out.

"You talked to Shari?"

I paused, not expecting her to say that. "Um, no. Shari? Did you talk to her? Did she say anything about me?"

Maggie paused. "You should call her."

Tears stung my eyes as I thought about our fight. Calling her was the last thing I could do. "She needs a break from me," I said softly.

"She needs a friend, Clem. She's going through something, and she needs you even if she's saying she doesn't."

A tear slipped down my cheek and I wiped it away. There was no reason for me to be crying. I'd hurt Shari. It was pathetic that I was responding in this way. "But..."

I was worried that what Maggie had said wasn't true. That Shari was doing just fine without me. That when I was in her life, I only ruined things for her.

"Trust me, she needs you. Now more than ever."

I appreciated how gentle Maggie was being with me. It helped lessen the stress that had cemented itself in my gut. "I'll keep that in mind."

"Well, act a little sooner than later, that's all I have to say, and we can leave it at that."

I nodded, and when I realized that Maggie couldn't see me, I responded with a yes. Maggie's laughter was soft as she told me she was done chastising me and asked me why I'd called.

"I got a loan approval," I said as the excitement that I'd

felt before she brought up Shari came flooding back. "I'm going to put in an offer to Max." I tipped forward, placing my feet on the ground in front of me as I drew circles on the counter.

Maggie cheered, and that was exactly what I needed to hear. Her excitement marching in time with my own.

"I'm so happy for you. You deserve this."

My smile was broader than ever before as I nodded. "I hope it works out. If I get this far only to lose the place to another buyer, I just might die."

"You won't. You'll get it. I promise. And then I'll take lessons from you, and you can teach me how to not have two left feet."

"Deal," I said.

Maggie sighed. "I gotta go. But call me later, 'kay? You can come over for dinner, and we'll celebrate. I found this amazing new chef that you have to try."

"I'll be there," I said. After saying our goodbyes, I hung up the phone. For a moment, my finger lingered above Shari's name as I contemplated calling her. But then I shook my head and scrolled down to Max's number.

I'd call Shari later when I had privacy and the mental capacity to handle everything.

I waited through a few rings before Max picked up. The butterflies in my stomach began to dive-bomb when I heard the rough sound of his voice.

"Hey, Clementine. I'm glad you called me because I was just searching for your number."

I fiddled with a stack of scrap papers in front of me.

"You were?" I asked as fear clung to my throat.

"Yep. I got the other offer in, and I want to move on this, so I was wondering if you'd heard back." He paused. "Did you hear back?"

"Yes, sir," I said as if that was going to help my chances. I doubted it would, but a girl could try.

"Great. Wanna tell me what it is?"

"I can offer you full list price." Last time I'd checked, he was asking three hundred thousand. That was well below what I'd been approved for, which left me with the money I had in savings to fix the place up. Anything over three hundred and I would be stretched pretty thin in terms of mortgage payment.

"Are you sure?"

I wanted to ask him what the other buyer offered, but I knew that he wouldn't tell me. So I gathered my courage and gave him a resounding yes. He laughed and told me that he would talk to his daughter and then get back to me with his answer.

I hung up the phone and set it screen down on the counter in front of me. Then I stretched out and sighed, the weight that had been crushing me felt a tad lighter. Like I just might actually be able to survive this situation with Shari and my desperation from living and working at a hardware store.

I stood and slipped off the stool and decided to focus my newfound energy on cleaning the store. The shelves needed to be wiped down, and the floor needed to be swept and mopped.

Not wanting to work in silence, I grabbed my phone, hooked it up to the speakers, and turned on my favorite Korean channel. Soon, I was dancing and singing along—even though I wasn't sure what was being said or if I was saying it right, I didn't let that hold me back.

Instead, I wailed into the broom handle at the top of my lungs. Singing and dancing without restraint does something to the soul. Heals it in a way that just talking can't. I felt lighter and lighter the more I danced and the harder I sang.

I didn't stop until I heard a very familiar chuckle from behind me. I startled and turned around to see Jake with a grin on his face. His brows were furrowed, and he was holding a plastic bag with containers from Shakes.

I danced up to him, still singing, and then launched myself into his arms. He caught me, wrapping his arms around me, and lifted me up to spin in a circle. I tipped my head back and laughed without inhibition.

For the first time in a long time, I felt free.

Jake lowered me down onto the ground, and we walked over to the register. He pulled out the containers and set them on the counter. I moved to grab one, but Jake pulled it back.

"Yours has no onions," he said as he nudged the other container toward me.

I nodded and moved to open it, shocked that he remembered that about me. He must have noticed the way that I was looking at him because he sighed and turned his attention to his food.

"I remember a lot, Orange." He wiggled his eyebrows as he said his most favorite nickname he came up with for me when we were kids.

I shook my head. It was ridiculous back then, and it was even more ridiculous now. "Har har," I said as I brought my burger up to my lips and took a bite.

He shrugged. "It works."

"No, it doesn't," I said as I tossed a french fry in his direction. He didn't even hesitate to catch it and slip it into his mouth. "Boo." In order to save face, I threw a cluster of three his way. He caught one with his mouth and one with his hand, but the other fell to the ground.

He grinned at me as he emphatically chewed the fry he'd caught in his mouth and then shoved in the other fry he'd caught after he swallowed that one.

I looked at him expectantly. "There's one more."

Jake glanced down at the ground and then back up at me. "I'm not eating that one," he said.

I parted my lips and scoffed. "Come on. I just cleaned that floor."

Jake studied me while he chewed and then sighed and bent down to retrieve the fry. He held it between his fingers, and I nodded toward his lips. "Anytime," I said.

Jake narrowed his eyes but then slowly moved the fry up above his mouth as if he were about to drop it in. I waited to see if he was really going to do it, but right before the fry touched his lips, I reached forward and snatched it from his fingers.

"Aww, you were going to drink the fat?" I asked in my best Rachel from *FRIENDS* impersonation.

He dropped his hand as he glanced over at me. "For you? Yep." And then he turned his attention to his burger as if he hadn't just said what he said.

I swallowed as emotions rose up inside of me. It scared me that he was so open and honest like this. What was I supposed to do with what he'd just said? How should I process it?

How could I ignore it?

Needing a moment, I excused myself and locked myself in the bathroom. Now alone, I turned on the faucet and allowed the cold water to run onto my fingers and over my hands. Then I splashed my face a few times before straightening and studying my reflection.

Water dropped from my nose and rolled down my cheeks, collecting on my chin. I turned my face side to side and allowed my thoughts to flow. Jake was flirting with me. We'd kissed last night. Things were moving faster than I'd anticipated, and it scared me enough to make me pull back and evaluate what I wanted to do.

My phone went off and snapped me from my reverie. I quickly dried my hands and fished it out of my back pocket. My heart took off racing when I realized that it was Max.

"H-hello?" I asked as I brought the phone up to my cheek.

"Clementine?"

"Yes?"

"Ah. It's Max."

"I know." I silently willed him to speak faster. I felt as if I were literally on the edge of my seat. In an effort to keep myself from collapsing from the stress, I leaned against the door and tipped my face up and closed my eyes.

"What's up?"

Max cleared his throat, and it was in that moment that I realized he was about to say something that I wasn't going to like. And it was as if my entire world had come crashing down around me.

Tears pricked my eyes as I waited for him to crush my dream of owning my own studio and finally doing something that I wanted to do. Because I knew it was coming.

"I'm really sorry, but Trinity and I decided to go with the other offer." Max's voice broke, and I could tell that this was a struggle for him as much as it was for me. And that broke my heart. I looked at Max like he was my own father, and the last thing I wanted was for him to hurt because of me.

"It's okay, Max," I said as I attempted to stifle my emotions and sound relaxed.

"Really?" he asked, and I hated how hopeful he sounded.

"Of course. I really appreciate you waiting for me to get the funding figured out. That was really above and beyond what most would do."

"Thanks, Clementine," he said.

I nodded even though tears were streaming down my face. "Of course. Enjoy retirement, and come and visit every so often. We'll miss you around here."

"I will. I've got a boat picked out and everything."

"Sounds amazing."

We said our goodbyes, and as soon as he hung up, I dropped my hand to my side while still clutching my phone. I closed my eyes and allowed the tears to flow. So much disappointment was wrapped up in that phone call that I doubted I would even survive.

I slid down the door and crouched with my forehead resting on my knees. A sob escaped as I squeezed my eyes closed. Maybe if I wished hard enough, I could will away all the pain that was cemented to my insides.

The pain from losing my best friend mixed with the pain of losing my dreams…again.

All I needed now was for Jake to walk away from me to essentially relive the past.

Jake.

I sniffled as I wiped my nose and dried my tears with a nearby paper towel. He was probably wondering what the heck I was doing. I moved to the sink, where I washed my hands and then patted my cheeks. If he asked if I had been crying, I'd just tell him that I had allergies. That would work, right?

I sighed, doubting my own story already. Even though it was lame, it was going to have to work.

I pulled open the bathroom door and headed out into the hallway. Just before I rounded the corner, Jake's voice caused me to stop. I stilled as I tipped my ear toward him and listened.

"Oh, man, that's just great. I'm happy you appreciated my offer."

I furrowed my brow as I leaned closer.

"Yep. I can meet you at the bank. Tomorrow works." He paused, and I waited, wishing I could hear whoever was on the other side. I had a sinking suspicion that I knew who it was, but I didn't want to jump to conclusions if it wasn't true.

"Yep. Noon works. I'll let Kevin know that we are coming over to sign the deed." He laughed, and the sound felt like daggers to my chest.

"I'll see you tomorrow, Max, and we'll make this all official."

It felt like a slap to the face even though I knew it was coming. Jake was the new owner of the building next door. He was going to build whatever company he wanted right in front of me. He was going to have his dream while I still struggled to obtain my own.

Too exhausted to think, I staggered from the corner that I was hiding behind and marched over to the register. No matter if Jake meant to do it or not, he'd broken my heart. Shari was gone, and now my dream was ruined. And yet again, the one person at the center of all of this was Jake. I should have known better than to let him back into my life.

"I think you need to go," I barely managed out. It was taking all of my strength not to break down into tears right in front of him. The last thing I needed was to turn into a sobbing, blubbering mess.

Jake raised his eyebrows. "I'm sorry?"

I shoved the Styrofoam containers into the bag he'd brought and then deposited that into the garbage. "I think you need to go," I said again, waving toward the front door.

Jake followed my motion with his eyes and then glanced back at me. "Oh, okay," he said as he slipped his phone into his back pocket and stood.

Just as he leaned forward to kiss me, I moved away, dropping my gaze to the ground. "About that," I said even though my heart felt as if it were shattering into a million pieces. "We can't do this again."

I paused, gathered my courage, and then glanced up to meet his gaze. The look in his eyes almost killed me as I saw him searching my face for an explanation.

"What?" he asked.

I swallowed and stood my ground. "We aren't going to do this again. We were stupid to think we could just pick up where we left off. I'm sorry." I marched over to the front door and pushed it open.

Jake stared at me as if he was completely confused. Then he shook his head. "No, Clementine. No. We are meant to be together." He neared me and reached out, but I pulled my arm back to keep him from touching me.

"I mean it, Jake. We're not going to start this up again." I sucked in my breath as I forced myself to be firm. "Please leave."

Jake studied me for a moment longer before he nodded. "Alright," he said as he walked past me and stood just outside the door. He slowly turned to face me. "I'm sorry for what I did."

I nodded but didn't wait for him to speak more. Instead, I turned and walked away from the door. I headed to the backroom. When I passed by Spencer's window, I called out for him to watch the front of the store for a moment.

I didn't wait for his normal grunt in response. I pushed through the door and collapsed onto the stairs. I buried my head in my hands and sobbed.

My entire body felt as if it were breaking as I realized that every dream I'd had was now dead, and yet I was still here to live a life I didn't want.

I was completely alone, and no matter what I did to change that, I was going to continue to be alone.

Forever.

SHARI

The house felt so strange. I got home to relieve Carol and discovered that Craig had already packed up most of his belongings. He didn't even wait to tell me where he was going, he was just gone.

That coward left me to tell the kids what was happening by myself. Which only made me hate him more. Bella broke down into tears, and Tag's face hardened and he stormed out of the living room and slammed his bedroom door.

It broke my heart to see my children react to this news. For a moment, I contemplated retracting my decision for the sake of my children, but I knew I couldn't. At some point in the future, we were going to find our new normal. And even though Craig and I didn't love each other anymore, I knew once he was settled, he'd make an attempt to be in their life.

He wasn't a bad father, and if he didn't have to sneak

around in his relationships, perhaps he would be able to finally focus on his children like he should.

At least, that was the outcome I chose to cling to, to help me get through the stress that our household was now under. I was having a hard time sleeping, and tears were my constant companion. Thankfully I had work to distract myself. At least when I was burying myself in parent complaints, I wasn't thinking about how my entire life felt as if it were constantly circling the drain.

By Wednesday, I was ready to call a truce on the fight with Jake and welcome him back into my messy life. I was tired of being alone, and even though it hurt that they'd ganged up on me, I knew I was going to have to forgive them at some point. After all, Jake was my brother, and Clementine felt like my sister.

Both of them were a part of my life that I was never going to lose, and I needed to act sooner than later if I wanted to keep it that way.

So I sent Jake a quick text, asking him to dinner, to which he responded with a thumbs-up. I slipped my phone into my purse and hurried Tag and Bella out of my office. I stopped by the take-and-bake pizza place and grabbed a few pizzas. I wasn't in the mood to cook, and I wanted to focus my attention on Jake and making sure I fixed what I'd broken.

When we got home, I started the oven preheating and then emptied Tag and Bella's lunch boxes and loaded the dishwasher.

As stressful it was to be alone now, there was a certain

freedom that came from the knowledge that I wasn't going to be waiting around for Craig anymore. I didn't have to wonder if he was coming home or not. It took the guesswork out of what I should expect for the day.

Plus, there was no more guilt around Jake coming over. I could finally have the relationship with my family that I'd given up to be married to Craig. And that thought helped lessen the stress I felt from my new status as a single mom—which, when I thought about it, crushed me with the weight of what that meant.

Which was why I was refusing to think about that. Instead, I was going to push it to the side for now.

The oven rang, indicating that it was time to slip the pizzas inside, just as Jake opened the back door and kicked off his shoes.

"Hey," I said as I adjusted the pizza on the stone and shut the oven door.

Jake raked his hands through his hair and nodded. "Hey," he said. His normal happy, smiling demeanor was gone, and it only made me more frustrated with myself.

Why had I taken so long to reach out to him? He was worried about me, and it made me angry that I'd left him hurting for so long.

So I didn't wait to cross the room and throw my arms around him. I pulled him into a tight hug. He remained still at first and then wrapped his arms around me and lifted me off the ground.

"I'm sorry," I said as he set me down. I peered up at him to see that a faint smile had returned to his lips.

"I'm sorry, too," he said.

I pulled back when I noted that he didn't seem relieved that I'd apologized. I furrowed my brow as I studied him. "So why are you still sad?"

Jake dropped his gaze to his hands and then glanced back up at me. He sighed. "It's been a crappy few days."

I nodded as I folded my arms across my chest and leaned against the counter. "Because of me?"

He shook his head then shrugged. "Well, slightly because of you. Like, ten percent."

I scoffed. "What was the other ninety percent?"

He paused before he glanced up at me and held my gaze. And then I knew what had him out of place. It was the same look he'd had when he left Magnolia for Anchorage.

"Clementine," I said softly.

Jake closed his eyes as his attempt to hide his pain was replaced with the pure agony that he felt. "Yes."

I sighed as I walked over to him and grabbed his hand. Then I led him over to the bar and pushed him down onto a stool. I grabbed the half-empty wine bottle from the fridge and retrieved two glasses from the cupboard.

After I poured us both a glass, I handed him one while holding the other in my hand. I took a sip and then turned to him. "Spill."

He studied me and then glanced around. "Where's Craig?"

Just like that, the realization that Craig was gone washed over me. Jake must have seen the change in my expression as he furrowed his brow. "Shari," he said in a way that told me he wasn't going to be satisfied until I told him what had happened.

So I did. I told him everything. When I got to the texts and the cheating, his eyes narrowed and he cursed under his breath, saying that if he ever saw Craig, things would not turn out well. I sighed as I gave him the *stay out of it* look. When I was finished, Jake stood and wrapped me into a crushing hug.

"I'm so sorry you had to go through that alone," he said as he pulled back.

I nodded as emotions rose up inside of my throat. "It's okay. It's not like I made it easy for you." I patted his back, and he pulled away to study me once more. "I'll be fine. I have you and Cl—" But as I started saying her name, I watched Jake's lips turn down and he moved back to sit on the stool. I folded my arms as I eyed him. "Tell me what happened."

Jake pushed around a few crumbs on the countertop with his fingertips. Then he sighed and peered up at me. "We kissed."

I wasn't surprised. "And?"

Jake studied me. "And I thought we'd moved on from the past. I told her I wanted to be with her no matter how long it took for her to want to be with me. Things were looking up until I went to eat lunch with her on Monday. She went to the bathroom and came back saying I needed to leave and she wanted nothing to do with me." He paused, pinching his lips and closing his eyes. He took in a deep breath and then let it out slowly.

He was hurting, and it made me frustrated for him. I hated seeing my kid brother in pain even though, most of the time, he brought things on himself.

"Okay, let's talk through this. I'm sure we can figure out what happened if you walk me through it."

Jake nodded. Then he relayed the story to me. He brought lunch over and they ate together. He thought everything was fine because she was flirting and laughing with him. Then she went to the bathroom. He got a phone call, and when she came back, she told him to leave.

I listened intently for anything that would clue me in to why Clementine would suddenly change her mind. Nothing stood out to me, which only frustrated me more. I wanted things to at least work out for my brother and my friend if they weren't going to work out for me.

By the time Jake finished, he looked at me in desperation. I furrowed my brow as I shook my head.

"I don't know what to tell you. I don't see what would have suddenly made Clem clam up like that." I tapped my finger with my chin. "Who called you?" That was the only piece of the story that he hadn't given me much detail on.

Jake's smile widened. "Oh, it was Max. He said I won the bid for his building. I'm going to open a small seafood restaurant that serves lobster rolls and such. Things that can be caught locally."

My hand fell to the countertop as I stared at him. My lips were parted and my mind was racing.

Jake must have been confused by my reaction because he stared at me. "What?" he asked.

"You're buying Max's store?" I needed to make sure I got the story right.

Jake nodded slowly. "Yes. Why is that such a shock?"

I sighed and scrubbed my face. "I think I know what happened."

Jake's eyes were wide and he looked desperate. "What?"

"You won the bid against Clementine," I said slowly.

Jake looked confused. "What?"

"Clementine. She put in a bid with Max as well. She wants to turn the place into a dance studio." I sighed as my heart went out to my friend. She must have been devastated. "She probably overheard your conversation and realized she wasn't going to be able to follow through on her dream." I folded my arms as I studied my brother.

He was staring off into the distance and I could see that he was chewing on my words. "That's why she was at the bank." His voice drifted off. "Why didn't she say anything?"

I shrugged. "She probably wanted to wait until she knew for sure. Why didn't you say anything to her?" I reached out and punched his arm.

Jake's hand flew up and he rubbed the spot I'd just hit. He glowered at me. "I was waiting for confirmation as well."

I scoffed, but before I could say anything, the timer rang. I walked over to the oven and peered in at the pizza.

The cheese was bubbling and the pepperoni was curling up on the sides. I grabbed my pizza paddle and pulled the pizza out.

Once it was on the counter and cooling and the other pizza was inside the oven, I turned to Jake and folded my arms. "So what are you going to do?" I asked.

Jake looked as stunned as ever, but I could tell that he was contemplating his plan. After a few seconds, it was like a lightbulb went off as he glanced over at me.

"I need your help," he said.

"With what?" When he got like this, it never made me feel good. It always involved me doing something that either endangered my life or left me physically scarred.

Jake waved away my fear as he stood and grabbed a piece of paper. "It won't be like that. It'll be so much better."

I parted my lips, but before I could speak, Jake started rattling off all the things he needed to do. It took a few items before I finally figured out his plan.

He was going to turn the space into a studio. It was his chance to do something for Clementine, and he wasn't going to botch it this time.

It made me happy to see my brother so dedicated to something. And it helped lessen the sting of my own relationship's failure. So, for the time being, I was going to dive headfirst into helping him win Clementine back.

And why wouldn't I? I had nothing to lose and had the distraction of his cause to gain.

And right now, that was what I needed to survive. A

purpose and a focus outside of my household. And this seemed like the perfect one.

He stayed a bit longer, but after dinner was eaten and the kids were sent off to bed, we said goodbye and I waved as he drove down the driveway. I turned off the lights in the house as I headed to my room to crawl into bed.

After brushing my teeth and slipping into my pajamas, I turned off the light and lay there under the covers, staring up at the ceiling fan above me.

So many thoughts swirled around in my mind as I lost myself to the rhythmic turns of the blades. It felt like, for so long, I'd been on my own type of Tilt-A-Whirl, spinning and spinning with no hope of getting off.

Now that the ride was over and I was standing with my two feet firmly on the ground, I found myself feeling relieved but also scared.

Scared that I didn't know what my future held.

Scared that I wasn't going to be enough for my children.

I wanted to say that I was strong enough to be the parent my kids needed, but I knew that a male figure was important, and I would never be able to be a father to Bella and Tag. I could only hope that Craig could get his life together enough to be the dad they needed.

I turned to my side as I held my stomach. Nerves made the butterflies in my stomach fly around spastically.

The best thing I could do was take everything one day at a time. Each day would get better than the next. And then at some point, I wouldn't hurt anymore. At some point, I would heal enough to finally be happy again.

And at some point, way off in the distant future, I might be able to find it in my heart to love once more.

At least, that was the hope.

And that was all I had besides my two beautiful children.

Hope.

CLEMENTINE

Just when I thought things couldn't get worse, they did. With Jake not around and me confining myself to the hardware store, I could pretend that my dream of opening a dance studio was still alive. Until Saturday morning came and the sound of hammers and saws could be heard from next door.

Reality came crashing down, and I was acutely aware that my life wasn't going to go in the direction that had brought me so much excitement.

And it sucked.

I hooked my phone up to the store's Bluetooth speakers and blared my music as loud as I could. A few Magnolia residents came in and looked at me strangely but thankfully didn't ask me to turn it down.

Instead, they bought the items they'd come in for and left, leaving me alone in my misery to deal with my disappointment.

Around noon, I felt as if I was going to lose my mind. So I called El Azteca for delivery and settled down on the barstool behind the register and pulled out the next book club read. I still had time until our next meeting, but if I didn't get a jump start on the book now, I was going to fall so far behind that I would be desperate to catch up. And, right now, I didn't want to put myself in that situation.

My nose was buried in the book when I heard the front doorbell jingle. But I didn't bother to look up. Instead, I called out, "Afternoon," while I turned the page.

When they didn't respond, I glanced up to see Shari coming my direction.

I dropped my book to the counter and hurried to stand. We hadn't talked in a week, and I was beginning to think that she was never going to forgive me. I'd wanted to call her, but commonsense told me that it was better to wait for her to reach out to me.

She had what looked like my El Azteca order in her hand, so I hoped that this was the truce I was looking for.

"Hey," I said as I furrowed my brow.

Shari gave me a soft smile as she set my bag down on the counter. "I hope you don't mind. I was there for lunch and overheard the order. I figured I'd bring it over to you."

I pulled the bag closer to me and nodded as I peeked inside. "Thanks."

"Don't worry, I didn't do anything to it," she said as she leaned forward and extended her hand toward the bag.

I laughed. "I'm not doubting you."

She chuckled. "Good." Then she glanced around. "Is this a good time to talk?"

I nodded as I opened up the bag of chips I'd ordered and popped the top off the salsa container. "Yep." No one was in the store, and she would have my full attention.

"Perfect." She sighed as she set her purse down on the ground. "Craig and I are getting a divorce."

I swallowed just as those words left her lips and I ended up inhaling a sharp chip in my haste. I hawked and coughed, my eyes watering. "Excuse me," I said as I took a long drink from my water bottle. A few seconds later, I turned to face her. "I'm so sorry," I rasped.

She laughed and shook her head. "That's fine. It was a shock to me too…But I think deep down I always knew. I was fighting it, but I feel better now that I've accepted my future." She handed me over a napkin and I graciously took it.

"Thanks," I said as I dabbed my lips.

She sighed. "I'm sorry."

Her words caught me off guard, and I wasn't sure what she meant. Was she sorry for what happened after Jake's party or for making me cough? Was I allowed to be hopeful in either direction?

"It's okay," I said, figuring that was the best route to take.

She shook her head. "No. I overreacted. You and Jake were just looking out for me, and I exploded." She leaned forward and patted my hand. "I should feel lucky to have a friend who cares so much." Her eyes filled with tears, and I could see the pain she'd been carrying around for so long.

I didn't hesitate as I rounded the counter and pulled her into a hug. When we both started crying, I realized that we were going to be fine. We each had our demons. We each had our issues. But what we had that would never change was our love for each other. We'd spent years cultivating our friendship, and nothing was going to take that away.

"Thanks for coming to talk to me. I was worried things were over for good," I said as I cleared my throat and swiped at my cheeks. Shari did the same, clearing her throat as she nodded.

"Thanks for forgiving me. I was worried you'd written me off as a crazy person."

I chuckled and shook my head. "Oh, I still think you're crazy, but it's a crazy that I'm okay with."

"Oh good," she said with a laugh.

We spent the next hour laughing and eating chips. There was a lighter air to Shari. She was still worried about the future, but I could tell the other things that had been weighing her down had lessened. Even though I knew nothing would ever go back to *normal*, it felt as if things were starting to look up, and I was going to cling to that for now.

Once the food was gone, Shari stood and wiped her hands on a napkin, all the while smiling over at me.

I furrowed my brow as I watched her. "What?"

She shook her head. "Nothing." She sighed. "I should go. Jake is watching the kiddos and I should relieve him."

Pain from her words hit me like a ton of bricks. She was heading over to Max's store. The place where I should be right now. The place that I was going to use to realize my dreams.

Not wanting to break down in front of her, I forced a smile and nodded. "That's awesome. Have fun."

Shari eyed me as she shouldered her purse. Just as she turned to walk toward the front door, she paused and turned to face me. "I forgot, I have a note for you."

Confused, I took the crisp white envelope that she handed me. There was nothing written on the outside, so I waited for her to leave before I stuck my finger under the flap and ripped it open.

A single notecard fell out, and I had to stoop down to pick it up. It was written in Jake's handwriting.

Tonight, 8pm. Meet me at Max's

I started at his words, feeling frustrated that he wanted me to go to the exact place that had broken my heart. He obviously didn't realize why I was upset with him. He wanted me to see his new store, and it was going to kill me.

I shoved the notecard back into the envelope and stuck it into the pages of the book I was reading. I wasn't going to go. I needed to protect myself and my heart right now. Walking into the belly of the beast was not the way to do that.

But, once 7:30 rolled around and I was closing the

store, I couldn't help but wonder what he wanted to talk to me about. And the truth was, we were going to be neighbors for a long time. If I didn't want it to be awkward, it was probably best to bury the hatchet.

Plus, I wanted to see what he was doing with the space. What kind of store was he going to open? It would at least help me deal with losing the building if he opened something that interested me.

So as soon as the door was locked, I hurried upstairs and changed. I tried to keep it casual with a light-pink summer dress and white sandals. I brushed my hair and left it to fall in soft waves around my shoulders.

I took a few deep breaths as I stared at my reflection and then nodded as I turned and walked from the room. A few minutes later, I knocked on the front door of the old hobby shop. Paper was covering the window, and as I waited, I attempted to peek through the openings to see inside.

But I couldn't catch a glimpse of anything.

The sound of the lock disengaging caused me to straighten and face the door. It opened and Jake stood on the other side. He was wearing a light-blue button-up shirt with a pair of dark jeans. His hair was styled in a way that looked as if he were headed to a date.

Strange.

My cheeks flushed as I glanced down at my dress and realized that he could say the same thing about me. I looked like I was going on a date rather than just a get-to-know-you party at the neighbors.

Not letting myself dwell on that, I gave Jake a smile as he stepped back and waved me in. I stepped into the building and glanced around.

Confusion filled my mind as I took in the candlelit dinner set up on a blanket that was spread out on some dark dance mats. My gaze went from the food to the floor-to-ceiling mirrors that lined the longest wall. Soft Korean ballads played on the speakers that dotted the ceiling.

Confused, I glanced back at Jake, who had shut the front door and had his hands shoved into his front pockets. "What is this?" I whispered. Jake was starting up a dance studio? When? How?

Jake couldn't dance.

"Is this a joke?" I asked as tears filled my eyes. If it was a joke, it was a mean one. Setting up the one thing that I wanted to open was a horrible joke. "Are you trying to hurt me?" My frustration at the situation began to rise, and I started to pace to help alleviate my agitation.

"What?" Jake asked, and his confusion just fueled me on.

"Why would you do this? Did you know that opening a studio was what I wanted to do? Is this your way of getting back at me?" My voice was higher now, and I hated how my feelings were exposed just through the sound of my voice. I turned away from him and buried my face in my hands.

Why was I so pathetic? I was officially losing my mind.

Before I could answer my own question, the feeling of

two arms surrounding me caused me to freeze. I stood there, my heart pounding in my chest as I pulled my face up and glanced behind me.

Jake was smiling as he studied me. He didn't even attempt to pull back, instead he tightened his grip on me.

"Silly, Orange," he said as he leaned into me.

I wanted to be angry, but I didn't know how to be. Instead I stood there, frozen to the spot, waiting for him to continue.

"I told you I was going to make up to you for what I did. I told you that I wasn't going anywhere." He leaned in and pressed his lips to my nose. "I had no idea that you were bidding for this place. If I had…" He let his voice drift off as he met my gaze and held it for a moment. Then he shook his head. "Actually, I would have bought this still."

I scoffed and moved to push him away. He just laughed and tightened his grip on me. He wasn't going to let me go, and if I were honest with myself, I didn't want him to.

"I bought this place with cash that I saved up over the years." He smiled down at me. "I wouldn't want you to mortgage your store and your life to open up a studio."

My eyes began to fill with tears as he spoke. I'd been alone for so long. And having someone else worry about these things along with me filled an empty hole that had existed in my heart for years. I found myself leaning into him as he spoke.

"I want to take care of you, Clementine. I want to help you fulfill your dreams. As soon as Shari told me that you wanted to turn this place into a dance studio, I knew I couldn't do anything else with this space."

I peered up at him to see him staring down at me with so much love that it took my breath away. I wanted to speak, but there were too many emotions racing through my body. And Jake seemed to notice that. He reached up and cupped my cheek, using his thumb to wipe away my tears.

"Will you let me take care of you?"

A sob escaped my lips when I attempted to speak, so I just nodded. He smiled as he dipped down and pressed his lips to mine. I wrapped my arms around his neck and pulled him to me.

He didn't release me. Instead, he just moved his hands down my body to my back and pulled me in close. We stood there, our lips moving in time with each other. This was what I was born to do.

Loving Jake wasn't something that I could just stop doing, and the years that we'd spent away from each other was proof of that. We were meant to be together. Fate knew this and that was why, despite all the twists and turns, we found each other once more.

At a time when we both needed what the other could offer, Jake and I were once again together. And this time, it was going to be forever.

Jake pulled back and met my gaze. "I love you," he whispered. His voice was so low and so deep that it sent shivers across my skin.

I met his statement with a smile as I nodded. "I love you, too," I said.

And with that, he pressed his lips to mine once more. We kissed without reserve. Our bodies were pressed so close together that it was hard to know where one ended and the other started.

Finally, we were together.

Finally, I felt as if my life could start.

With Jake by my side, I knew I was going to be able to face anything. He was mine and I was his, and for now, that was all that mattered.

I finally felt like I'd come home. I finally felt like I belonged.

Here, in Magnolia.

***

I hope you enjoyed A Magnolia Homecoming. Shari and Clementine were so fun to write about. I loved diving into Shari's story and how it was such an integral part in Clementine's road to love.

I am SO excited to write Shari's pathway to self-acceptance and love in A Magnolia Friendship. The romance I have in store for her is going to be EPIC! Plus, we get to learn more about Victoria, the town's mayor and discover why she is the way she is.

And how she's about to lose her job.

Head on over to your favorite platform to grab you copy today HERE!

I would love for you to join my newsletter so you don't miss out on any new release, PLUS get a FREE novella on me! Click HERE or if you are reading via paperback, place your phone camera over the QR code to get signed up!

If you missed The Magnolia Inn, the first book in the Red Stiletto Book Club Series, make sure to grab it HERE!

ALSO, if you enjoyed reading about Scarlet, I have a recently released NOVELLA that focuses on just her romance.
There are two ways of acquiring her story.
You can purchase it on your favorite retailer
HERE

I also have a complete family saga series that I'm sure you would love! Read the first in the Braxton Brother's Romances, HERE!

Coming Home to Honey Grove with make you swoon, cry, and sigh.

Joshua is back in Honey Grove. As a divorced, single dad, he's decided that love is the last thing he needs.

Beth is back in Honey Grove after losing her job and getting dumped.

When Josh's mother, the town's busy body, arranges for Beth to be his nanny, Josh decides to go along with the plan.

Even though Beth is no longer the lanky girl next door, Josh isn't looking for a relationship anyway. He can keep her at a distance. Right?

Everything seems to be working out until their relationship deepens and their arrangement isn't enough anymore.

Too bad her feelings for Josh isn't Beth's only secret.

If you want to connect with Anne-Marie Meyer, join her newsletter and receive Fighting Love with the Cowboy for FREE!

Sign up HERE!

Also join her on these platforms:
Facebook
Instagram
anne-mariemeyer.com

Printed in Great Britain
by Amazon